Her Long Walk Home

LINDA BARRETT

DEDICATION

The story is dedicated to the City of Boston, 2013,
For showing the world the meaning of Boston Strong.

Athletes ran, crowds cheered, three innocents died and
scores were injured. Citizens rallied and officials organized.
You came through.

A year later, athletes ran, crowds cheered, and
memories lingered.
Forever April. Forever Marathon. Forever Boston
Strong.

Cover art by Rogenna Brewer

www.sweettoheat.blogspot.com

E-book and print formatting by Web Crafters

www.webcraftersdesign.com

Copy Editing by Amy Knupp

www.blueotterediting.com

CHAPTER ONE

"Will she use the ramp or try the stairs?"

Bartholomew Quinn, proud founder and co-president of Quinn Real Estate and Property Management, leaned forward in his oversized leather chair and peered through the large front window of his Main Street office. A young woman faced the building, her dark hair neatly gathered behind her neck. She wore a long dark skirt and a red sweater. In her right hand, she held a cane. Bart watched her glance flicker between the two paths. Ramp or stairs? Either might be considered a challenge for her, but… He caught her determined expression as she made her choice.

Quickly transferring the cane, the woman placed her right hand on the railing. Her chin jutted forward as she raised her right foot to the first step, her left following only a tad more slowly.

"Atta girl," he cheered.

Quinn had become familiar with this girl's background through a trustworthy friend. Now he'd seen her in action for himself. In a moment, he'd depend on his gut instinct to fill in the blanks. He'd been blessed with the knack, those "people skills" folks talked about, and those instincts had never let him down. He'd know Rebecca Hart well by the time their conversation was over.

A sea breeze brought the flavor of the ocean to Bart's nose, and he inhaled with joy. Another summer season was poised to begin in Pilgrim Cove, his favorite place on earth. He'd spent his entire adult life here, and he'd be buried here—God willing—many years from now. He was young! Seventy-six years young, and people in this town depended on him.

He and his buddies had come through every time. They made themselves available to meet, greet, and befriend newcomers as well as summer folk. Or, as his granddaughter Lila would say, they were always ready to meddle—especially him. Well, his lassie might have a point. But he wasn't so sure. So far, all his "meddling" had turned out well.

And now, Rebecca Hart had come to see him. His anticipation sizzled as he walked down the hallway to greet her. Hopefully, Sea View House would be sheltering a new resident.

#

Becca hid her smile as she evaluated Bart Quinn. The old guy had definitely kissed the Blarney Stone more than a few times, but he still had it—that courtesy of his generation. A true gentleman. He'd put her at ease immediately and treated her as though she were like anyone else. As though she hadn't been watching the runners at the finish line in Boston instead of running herself. As though the marathon had never happened. Except, of course, it had, and she wasn't one to wear rose-colored glasses. Leaning across Quinn's desk, Becca stared directly at him, commanding his full attention.

"My cousin, Josie, and I checked into the Wayside Inn last night, but I can't afford to stay there much longer. So I'd like to see this house you have where the rent is so reasonable it has to be a mistake." If there was a mix-up, she'd need to find another place right away. "My graduate professor at BU insisted I contact you. He said his colleague at Harvard had some clout with this office. Is that true?"

The light in Quinn's blue eyes rivaled the light of the sun. It sparkled and blazed as he rubbed his hands together. Becca sat hypnotized. Was Quinn a man or an oversized leprechaun? His fist banged the arm of his chair.

"You're talking about Daniel Stone! We call him the Professor. Comes back every year since his first summer in Pilgrim Cove. Now that was a story... Was it last year or the one before that, when he stayed at Sea View House? He'd lost his wife, ya see, and was in a grievous state." Quinn's head moved from side to side as he made sorrowful sounds. "I gave him the upstairs apartment, the Crow's Nest. But waiting for him downstairs was Shelley Anderson and her two little tykes. Ahh. That was no ordinary summer, no sirree. And now they're a family, everybody together."

His index finger pointed directly at her. "Sea View House holds the magic."

Magic? Baloney. She'd bet her last nickel the man could regale her with stories until the sun went down. She didn't have time for stories.

"Very nice, Mr. Quinn. But what I need to know is whether you've got a cottage for me to rent this summer. Easy access would be needed."

"True enough, lassie. But you did well coming up those steps. I watched from that window." He pointed behind him.

Her body stiffened. "You spied on me?" She adjusted her angle slightly to peer over his shoulder. Sure enough, she saw a swath of Main Street through the glass. She looked at Quinn again and sighed. "Why am I not surprised? I bet you don't miss much around here."

"You'd win that bet, my girl. This town is special to me. And will be to you, too."

"You mean you've got a place for rent? A house that will suit me?"

"Haven't you been listening, lass?"

He posed the question with such wide-eyed innocence that her lips twitched. Between the irascible Bart Quinn and her own one-track mind, she was in no better position than Alice was in Wonderland. The twitch became a smile, then a giggle, and she found herself laughing aloud, as though she'd finally gotten the joke.

And then the tears fell.

She reached for the tissue box Quinn slid toward her and dabbed her eyes. Strange that she wasn't embarrassed. "Well, that was a first."

"The laughing?"

"No. The crying."

The man seemed surprised.

"They have meds for the physical pain, Mr. Quinn. No tears there. As for the rest, well, as my mother taught me from the beginning: *Life hurts. Deal with it.*"

After studying her for a moment, Bart Quinn finally said, "Well, now, respecting all mothers, of course, I've got a different slant. I say, *Grab the brass ring and enjoy the ride."* He rose from his seat, rummaged through a drawer, and soon dangled a set of keys. "Let's go, my dear."

"Go where?"

"Where else would I bring a friend of a friend of Daniel Stone's than to Sea View House? Right beside the ocean, where you'll hear the sound of the surf, the call of the gulls, and where you'll find your own healing."

#

Becca was about to tell him that her healing came from physical therapy, not from ocean waves, when two small tornadoes blew into the room. The first was blonde, her long hair woven into a French braid that probably started the day neatly plaited. The other whirlwind sported dark waves framing a sweet face. Cinderella and Snow White. Totally adorable.

"Guess what, Papa Bart!" said Cinderella. "No school till Tuesday 'cause of the holiday, so Sara can sleep over." The child's infectious grin coupled with her attitude easily confirmed her as a twig on Bart Quinn's family tree.

Sara stepped forward. "If that's okay," she added quietly.

This girl's entrance had been embellished by her friend. Sara seemed more reserved and sensitive. A classic dark-eyed beauty who'd mature into a stunning woman one day.

"Sara, my girl," began Bart, "would you condemn me to a quiet house when we could be playing a hot game of…of"—Quinn glanced at Becca then back at the child—"Candy Land instead?"

5

A frown lined Sara's brow. "Candy Land?" she asked, her voice laced with incredulity. "That's for babies. Poker is more fun. Isn't your penny jar still full?"

Quinn looked at the ceiling, then at the girls. "Ach. What will Ms. Rebecca think of us now? You've gotten us in trouble, you have." He looked at Becca. Two other pairs of eyes followed suit. "Better a round of cards than leaving them to their little computer machines all night. Agree or not?"

Oh, she agreed. These children couldn't appreciate their good luck. A loving grandfather, probably good parents, too. Even the quieter one knew she was welcome here in the middle of a business day. Secure, confident children. They'd have no idea how other kids lived. Kids who hoarded a penny. Kids with no dads or granddads. Kids with a mom who worked all the time. Kids like Becca.

She couldn't have found better entertainment than Bart Quinn and the girls if she'd paid for a ticket of admission. But she hadn't come to be entertained. She tapped her watch. "Your granddaughters are delightful," she said. "But time is flying." Bracing her hands on the arms of the chair, she stood, took a moment to find her balance, and reached for her cane. "I'm ready when you are."

"I've been ready since the day I was born," said Quinn. Turning toward the little blonde, he said, "Katie, love, tell your mom I'm away to…"

A pretty blonde woman, definitely Katie's mom and definitely pregnant, walked into the room at a good clip, a leather tote bag on her arm.

"Wherever it is," she said, "you'll have to take the girls. I'm showing the Bascomb property on the bay, and then I've got a doctor's appointment, which I must keep or feel Jason's wrath."

"If you don't mind," said Becca, "I'll be waiting in my car—right out front." She'd have considered another Realtor at this point if her curiosity about Sea View House hadn't been piqued. Not to mention that low, low rent. And if she'd known another Realtor. The kids were cute, but really, was this any way to run a business?

As if she read her thoughts, the other woman smiled and extended her hand. "Hi there. I'm Lila Parker, Chief Cook and Bottle Washer around here. Where's my granddad taking you today?"

Becca shook her hand, glad to see no sign of pity or sympathy. "He calls it Sea View House."

Lila's brows hit her hairline, her eyes widened to saucer size, but a small grin started to emerge, too. "Perfect. It's a special place." She cocked her head toward Bart. "He's in charge of that property, never tells me about possible residents. It's all hush-hush until it's done."

Becca didn't care about mysteries, but walking was easier than standing, and she stepped toward the door. "I'll let you know how special it is…if I ever get there."

"I hear ya." Bart and the girls followed her. Once outside, the man installed the kids into the backseat of his decade-old Lincoln Town Car and opened the front passenger door for Becca.

"Honestly, Mr. Quinn, it's easier for me to drive. That is, to get into the car on the driver's side. My right leg's fine."

"Then I'll keep you in my mirror. We'll take it slow so you can look around as we travel."

Becca opened her door and threw her purse inside. She'd left the seat in the far back position she'd used to exit the car. Now she'd have enough room to manipulate her prosthetic left leg while getting in. She sat down facing the street, then turned and shifted her weight toward the front, her right leg going inside. She guided the left. The sequence made sense. Her physical therapy was paying off, and she'd be continuing it in Boston and at the medical clinic in Pilgrim Cove. If this house worked out. Or if Quinn had something else.

With a little luck, forethought, and care, she'd become the woman she once was. She'd become whole again. Or almost. Whole enough for a marathon? Whew. If only… She chased the thought away. More important on the survival scale was a job. As a respiratory therapist at Mass General, she'd needed strong legs to run around the halls, treating patients on every floor. She'd been building a career at the prestigious hospital, with two promotions behind her and supervisory responsibilities on her plate, too.

Now her small savings would trickle away in no time. There was a tiny chance, of course, that she'd receive some money from that charity fund set up after the marathon. But how much could that be? A few dollars? Even a few thousand wouldn't make a real difference in the long run. She'd have to rely only on herself. Her finances were tighter than a balloon's knot. A reality that tied her stomach into a dozen knots.

As promised, Quinn drove slowly, providing her with that opportunity to look around. From the man's office on Main Street, she passed a bank, a barber shop, and the nautically designed Diner on the Dunes. She spotted Parker Plumbing and Hardware. The name seemed familiar. That Lila woman? Then she saw the beautiful greyhound—on a leash. She glanced up. At the other end of the leash stood a tall, built, nice-looking guy. Behind the pair was a pet store with a big sign in the window. Adoption Day. Whew! A greyhound. Talk about running…

She followed Bart left onto Outlook Drive and made another left onto Beach Street. He tooted his horn, pointed out the window, and eased into a driveway.

Becca slowed down, scanned the street, and took her time before pulling in behind him.

She hadn't known what to expect, but Sea View House was bigger than anything she'd imagined or could care for. Salt-box style. Weathered wood. A large sloping roof. Two stories with a third window above…maybe an attic. A white wooden fence surrounded the front yard on Beach Street.

Disappointment flooded her. What was the man thinking? She could never take care of a house like that. She hoped Quinn had another property to show her. Something small and easy. She rolled down her window and remained inside the car. With her first breath, she tasted the flavor of ocean and sea grass. She inhaled again, more deeply this time. No mistaking that definitive aroma existing only at the shore.

She looked again at the big house. A house right on the beach. Not that she'd swim… How could she? But she'd hear the waves. She'd see them, too. And that view…the pleasure of that view…that elusive horizon where ocean meets sky. Tempting. Oh, so tempting. So different from the confines of a hospital rehab wing, where she'd spent the last five weeks working to recover.

"Needing some assistance after all, lassie?" Quinn was at her car door.

"What else do you have to show me?"

And with that question, she'd reduced Bart Quinn to silence.

#

So what if she'd jumped to conclusions? The house was divided into two apartments, as Quinn had mentioned in his story of the professor. The Realtor had the first floor in mind for Becca. While Sara and Katie scurried ahead, Becca walked more slowly down the paved driveway to the back of the house. And came to an abrupt halt when she saw the ocean. The mighty Atlantic would be her closest neighbor. Not a rabbit hole, this time. Paradise.

She noted the spacious covered porch leading to a big, grassy backyard. The yard ran to a low cement wall placed at the sand line. Inserted into the wall were tall boards. Something she'd never seen before.

"We'll remove those, of course," said Bart, "now that summer's here. But they're handy protection for the house when winter winds blow the sand around."

"Makes sense," said Becca. "Not that I have any experience living at the beach."

"Then you're in for a treat this season. You'll come to love our peninsula with the ocean on one side and the bay on the other. There's always a breeze here. Know what I call this place?" His eyes gleamed, and he gestured widely to incorporate his world. "I call it our finger in the ocean."

He made life in Pilgrim Cove sound like a fairy tale, but Becca held back. Despite an easy ferry commute north to Boston, this paradise posed other challenges. Walking on soft sand was just the beginning. But…with the shady back porch, she could simply step outdoors and feast her eyes on the entire breathtaking scene. The ever-changing sky. The moody ocean. And the busy beach. No more living cooped up in a city apartment three stories above the street. The place she shared with Josie had no elevator, and remaining there was not an option. Compromise. Life was now about compromise.

"We'll have the porch furniture out here in a jiffy," said Bart as he unlocked the door. "And anything else that needs to be done."

Wide-planked oak floors ran throughout the house, chintz-covered couches and chairs, and in the kitchen, ample counter space. Three bedrooms. Three! Well, Josie and her boyfriend could visit—an easy enough trip from Boston. She hoped her mom would visit, too, maybe stay for a week or more, but she didn't count on it. Angela had missed work after the marathon. She lived in the western part of the state near the Berkshires and had stayed in Becca's apartment while Becca was in the hospital. She probably had no vacation days left and for sure would never sacrifice a day's pay.

Becca shrugged. She was on her own in Pilgrim Cove. *Deal with it.*

"We'll install the grab bars in the shower and anything else you think you'd need. Maybe a tall stool at the counter here? Easier to sit and stand again." Quinn paced the kitchen, looking for possibilities. "Would that suit?"

Suit? Becca's heartbeat quickened as she looked around. Outside, she'd have the sun, sea, porch, and a steady breeze. But inside this weathered ship, she'd be surrounded by sturdy walls, a cozy fireplace, and wide halls—with elbow room. No problem using a cane or wheelchair. Sea View House. An island of safety. And privacy. She'd get stronger here and return to normal. Oh, yeah. It would suit.

"How much, Mr. Quinn?"

He jumped back as if she'd slapped him. "How much, lassie? Why there's no charge for Sea View House. Not for you. This beauty is let on a sliding scale, part of the William Adams Foundation, who was shirttail cousin to John Adams, himself, and wasn't he the second president of the United States?"

The man spoke faster than she could hear, but she got the part about "no charge." She didn't buy it.

Everything in life had a price. "Would you repeat that more slowly—about the rent?"

"No rent for you. The sliding scale, you see. By unanimous vote of the Board of Directors, of which I'm president."

Unbelievable. "Just to be clear, Mr. Quinn. Are you saying that this beautiful house—at least the first floor— is rent-free for the entire summer?"

"The first floor is called the Captain's Quarters, and that's exactly what I said, Ms. Rebecca. Rent-free. The question is, what do you say?"

"I say, where do I sign?"

Quinn laughed his big laugh. "Not to worry. I'll bring the papers around after you move in. I'll also bring the Sea View House journal, where you'll write your story."

Ahh. She knew there had to be a catch. "I'm no writer. Besides, the bombing's been in all the newspapers."

"Grammar doesn't count, girl! But stories do. It's a record, you see, about finding the magic again. You'll be able to catch up on all the folks who've stayed here before you. Like that professor you mentioned from Harvard who lived upstairs. Some other folks who've stayed here live in town now. In Pilgrim Cove. You'll probably meet them soon."

Not interested. Becca stared into the man's eyes, her gaze demanding his undivided attention. "Let's be perfectly clear, Mr. Quinn. My goal is to work hard and get strong enough to support myself later on—when I figure out how. I'll write something for you, but I'm not here to make friends or socialize. I had plenty of company in town after…after the explosions. Lots of attention and therapy. Sometimes too much. They were wonderful. Terrific people. But sometimes the hospital and the rehab center seemed like a madhouse to me.

Now I need to be independent. On my own. Do you understand?" She wouldn't put it past him to send a few neighbors over just to stir things up.

"We'll do all we can to help you," said Bart. "Modifications and all. You'll be able to move in tomorrow."

Logistically perfect, but she sighed. He hadn't acknowledged a word about her wanting to be left alone.

#

Friday night and child-free. Adam Fielding, DVM, locked the door to his veterinary clinic, his newest retired greyhound at his side, and wondered what to do with his unexpected leisure time. Evening was a killer. The loneliest time of the day, the time when memories of Eileen were the strongest. Her laughter…that dimple tucked beside her sweet mouth… He'd loved pressing kisses against it. He missed cuddling on the couch, playing with her dark, curly hair, wrapping the strands around his fingers. Sara had inherited that feature. He missed Eileen's intelligence—her fast quips and thoughtful suggestions, a strong support for a debt-ridden young veterinarian just starting out. He yearned for his loving wife, his perfect wife. The perfect woman for him. He spoke to the grey.

"Neptune Park's probably opened for the season, but I'll save the carousel and Ferris wheel for Sara."

Ginger whined in agreement. Adam leaned over and scratched behind her small, folded-back ears. "Of course, Katie will come along." The intelligent dog, parti-colored with a white background and fawn patches, tilted her head, listening to Adam's every word. After a month with him and Sara, the dog had adapted well to being a house pet and was ready to adopt out. But Sara had other ideas for the pretty canine.

"No, Daddy. Not this one. She's special. I love her. Please…"

His daughter didn't have to beg. He'd give her the moon if she asked for it. As for the greyhounds…they were all special, at least to him. Each one faced a huge adjustment after living in a kennel since birth and after a life at the track. As he'd done with others, Adam had taken Ginger home from the rescue center in Boston, helped her to adjust to family living—house, car, kids, stairs, bed—until she'd be ready for a permanent family.

He shrugged. So now they'd have another personal pet. No problem. Dogs and cats got along, and the mighty Butterscotch ruled his roost with confidence. Sara's devotion to Ginger was odd, though. His daughter normally used her energy and wits finding good homes for abandoned pets. She knew they couldn't keep every rescue brought into the clinic. It seemed, however, Sara and Ginger had an understanding. They were a twosome. From his observation, Sara's love for the grey was being returned twice over.

Love. Easier between a dad and daughter or between a child and a puppy than between a man and a woman. He'd tried romance again after Eileen, a sensible relationship with Katie's mom. But they'd called off the engagement after Jason Parker returned to Pilgrim Cove. With one glance at Jason's love-stricken expression when he'd looked at Lila, Adam had recognized his own yearning for Eileen. He'd bowed out. Gracefully, too. And never looked back.

But their daughters remained inseparable—sisters of the heart. And now Jason and Lila were expecting a sibling for Katie. He wished them well. Sometimes, everything worked out, especially when no one harbored any grudges.

He meandered next door to the house he shared with his daughter and her changing menagerie. His stomach rumbled when he went inside, but he had no appetite for cooking or being alone. The Friday night Happy Hour and dinner at the Wayside Inn would suit. He'd probably run into a few friends or neighbors and have a congenial time. A perfect evening.

No more romantic involvements for him. He'd focus his energies on being the best dad a little girl could have. Between caring for Sara, running his animal hospital, and planning the addition of a greyhound rescue and fostering center, he'd hardly be lonely or bored.

The rescue expansion excited him. The start-up funding came from his own savings and a bit from the Boston Greyhound Foundation, where he volunteered his services. He was waiting for word about other funding, a big chunk, from a state-sponsored animal foundation. Life was good. Good enough, anyway.

After a quick shower, he slapped on some cologne, grabbed a clean jersey and jeans, and headed out.

#

Thirty minutes later, Adam stood at the bar, nursing a longneck with Rachel and Jack Levine. The couple had married recently and decided to live in Pilgrim Cove, Rachel's hometown.

"I didn't realize the Inn would be this crowded," said Rachel. "We were trying to avoid the hordes at the Lobster Pot tonight."

The Wayside Inn boasted a restaurant, bar, dance floor, spacious lobby, and guest rooms while somehow retaining the picturesque New England flavor at the same time.

"The summer season's the money season," Adam said.

"On a holiday weekend, every place is crowded," said Jack. "We should've stayed home."

"Well, I'm glad you didn't," said Adam. "My daughter's with Katie, so I'm on my own."

"Maybe not for long." Rachel grinned and inclined her head toward two attractive brunettes several seats down the bar. "New in town. No gold bands. Let's welcome them to Pilgrim Cove." She shifted from her stool, starting to match action to her words.

"Whoa, Nelly! You're not the welcoming committee." Jack wrapped his arm around his wife, stopping her descent, and Adam breathed a sigh of relief. The man had his back, whether he realized it or not. Adam had no desire for small talk with strangers.

"Why not?" protested Rachel. "We're in Pilgrim Cove, not Manhattan. It's the start of summer, and everyone's on vacation and in a good mood. In another month, I will be, too."

"Some of us," drawled Jack, "work twelve months a year. Like Adam and me."

While the couple bantered, Adam glanced at the two women, who were now following a hostess toward a table. His brow narrowed. Something was off, and he continued to track their progress.

"The prettier one's got trouble. Big trouble," he muttered just as the woman turned toward him, head on an angle. She met his gaze, and her chin rose. Her brown eyes turned the shade of bitter cocoa, and as swiftly as she'd engaged him, she showed him her back.

Adam burned. Whether from embarrassment or anger, he couldn't discern. He couldn't think! The woman's eyes were as dark as Eileen's, her hair as chestnut brown and wavy as Sara's.... He needed air.

#

"The last thing I expect or need is to be hit on. Did you see that guy?" Becca leaned across the table toward her cousin. "But I think I scared him off."

"Sure, I saw him," said Josie. "Hard to miss Tall, Hazel, and Handsome. Easy on the eyes. But he was all about you, cuz. That is so cool!"

Meeting a nice guy in a bar might have been cool in the old days—not that this guy seemed "nice" at all. He'd studied her like a specimen on a Petri dish, and she wouldn't put up with that. If she ran into him again, she'd say so. But more important was the big picture. Today began her new tomorrow. The old days were gone.

"I don't need anyone in my life, Josie. I'm not in the market for pity or being second best. I'd rather be alone."

"Oh, please." Josie waved away her protestations as if slapping a gnat.

"You're only second best in your own mind. That guy was looking and looking hard."

"Until he saw me walk."

"You're imagining things."

But she hadn't imagined that. He'd stared at her so hard she'd felt the burn. And then she'd met his gaze and given as good as she'd gotten. She'd be willing to bet her bottom dollar—which was about all she had—that the only looks she'd receive from now on were those of curiosity and pity. Her hands clenched into fists. Not for her! She'd deal with those men like she'd dealt with Tall, Hazel, and Handsome tonight. Just return their stares with one of her own.

\#

As though Bart Quinn really was King of the Elves, the necessary modifications to her apartment started the very next day. Bart himself was overseeing the changes, the two children at his side. Furniture was moved, nonslip mats were placed under rugs, and grab bars were installed in the walk-in shower along with a plastic chair. Grab bars went on the wall by the tub, too.

These conveniences were essential. She had jotted notes to herself about the adjustments she'd need, but she wondered aloud how Bart Quinn had figured them out.

"Papa Bart knows everything," said Katie with a hard shake of her head and satisfaction in her voice. "That's what Grandma always says."

Bart's laughter had Becca joining in. "Not quite, lassie. But I like your version better. My daughters would say I just *think* I know everything."

"There's a difference," said Becca, smiling as she glanced from Katie to her loyal shadow. Sara leaned against "Papa Bart" as though she belonged to him, also. Sensitive. Lonely. Something was going on inside the sweet girl. Becca looked away. Not her business.

"Bart's friends are amazing, too," Josie said as they watched the house fix-it operation progress. "All sharper than their age."

"I agree," said Becca. "The shoemaker had his elves, but we have the ROMEOs. And the name fits them. These Retired Old Men Eating Out have the energy of guys ten years their junior. You'd think they owned the town the way they talk about it."

Rick O'Brien, retired police chief, had come to assure her that Sea View House had withstood many a hurricane and not to worry. He provided several flashlights and a supply of batteries. The electrician, Ralph Bigelow, had already guaranteed that her air conditioning wouldn't let her down. She'd thanked him but really wanted a sea breeze! And then came Doc

Rosen. Retired or not, the man had eyes that missed nothing. He could be an incredible ally.

"I know everyone at our community hospital," he'd said, "including the physical therapists in Outpatient. You call me with any question that comes up."

"Thanks," she said. "I hope to lead a very quiet life here. No emergencies, please. And I'll be taking most of my P.T. in Boston at the rehab center. I'm using the ferry service." She grinned. "Who knew people commuted by ferry? It'll be fun." If she didn't lose her balance when the boat rocked.

"Excellent! But my offer stands. If you need support in any way, you call us. My wife…my wife is a breast cancer survivor. We know about long-term treatment, timely treatment. We know personally how important it is to have people in your corner."

She struggled to find words. She'd never known men like these. They didn't know her but for two days, so why would they care so much? Her own dad…she'd barely known him. He'd died much too young, when she was only five years old. So what did she really know about dads and granddads? Not much.

Time to discover if these guys meant what they said. She walked through the center hall toward the bedrooms. "My first decision is about exercising. Dr. Rosen, which room would you choose as the best place for doing home therapy?"

"How wide is your mat and how wide are these beds?" asked the doctor. "The mat needs to be centered, not sticking out over the sides." He peered into the first guest room.

"More company's coming!" Josie's voice rang through the house, a voice tinged with excitement.

"Knock, knock." Another voice. This time mellow, deep, and definitely male.

CHAPTER TWO

A ROMEO would have just walked in. No shyness in that group. "I'll be right back," said Becca.

Doc Rosen nodded and continued examining the room. Watching out for her. She released a big breath as relief spread from head to toe, catching her by surprise. Ridiculous! She had a great team in Boston. She'd made all the arrangements for treatment before coming here. She'd been helped by scores of supportive medics after the bombing. They'd cheered for her and the others who'd been hurt. Heck, they'd all cheered each other on. Now she was ready to make it on her own. So why was she so glad about Doc Rosen's concern?

Sighing, she grabbed her cane, made her way back to the kitchen, and stopped short. All thoughts of therapy and doctors flew away. A man. A familiar man, this time with a dog almost as big as she was. What the h…?

He froze when he spotted her, seemed to be as surprised as she was. Then he smiled. And it was a lovely smile. Warm and friendly. But the glance he'd given her the night before at the Wayside Inn still stung.

This guy was not her friend, and the best defense was an offense.

"Who are you, and why are you stalking me?"

His brows lifted, and he glanced at Bart. "She must be one of your special cases for Sea View House. And a hard one at that, so good luck—to both of you. Now, where's Sara?"

Bart gave a careless wave of his hand. "Out and about. So, I see you two have already met…?"

Becca should have been used to the old man by now. Nothing escaped him. Nothing.

Her visitor had relaxed the dog's leash, and whether Becca wanted the animal to or not, the lovely greyhound stepped closer, examined Becca up and down, sniffed at the cane, and whined. The hound looked at its man, then continued around the cane, sniffing and examining before returning to Becca's accessible side and sitting.

Becca liked dogs in a general way, and automatically scratched this one behind the ears. However, she'd never owned a dog, either as a child or an adult. Her mom hadn't wanted more responsibility or expense, and Becca knew better than to nag.

"She's a retired racer," began the man.

Like me. Dampness covered her skin. Tears pressed behind her eyes. She took a breath, didn't want to believe her mind went back there, and was stunned how an unexpected phrase could revive that horrible day. *Think positive.*

"But we're alive." A non sequitor. Becca quickly pressed her lips together. She was awkward about everything recently, including conversation. The man's quizzical expression proved it. As if the prior evening hadn't been enough.

"Alive you are, my lass!" said Bart. "And we're grateful for it." He looked from one to the other. "To celebrate Rebecca's arrival in Pilgrim Cove, you'll both join me at the Lobster Pot tonight. Sara, too. Everyone will want to meet you, Rebecca, m'girl. You're a hero. In Pilgrim Cove, everyone's family, and there's no place to hide."

#

Bart Quinn was still up to his old tricks. One look at this new woman and Adam could see she was overwhelmed, shaking her head as the words came out of Bart's mouth. *But we're alive.* So maybe she really did have need of the Sea View House remedy. The magic. A lot of bull, but Bart believed it. In the meantime, Adam would help her out. Besides, he liked the way she rubbed Ginger behind the ears. The dog was on the verge of swooning.

"Don't let Bartholomew boss you around," he said in a conspiratorial tone. "Stand up to him!" Ow. He winced at his bad choice of words.

Her dark eyes flashed. "I can *stand up* to anybody, including you. Whoever you are."

"Adam Fielding," he said, offering his hand. "Sara's dad. I run a veterinary clinic not a half mile away from here."

"Rebecca Hart." She peered more closely at him. "Veterinary? Weren't you standing on Main Street yesterday, in front of the pet shop?" She looked at Ginger. "But not with this dog."

"I work with the local greyhound association, trying to place these wonderful racers into good homes. Yesterday was Adopt-a-Pet Day, so I was there."

"Did she find a good home?"

"Not yet. She's back with her foster family, but we'll keep trying."

And that's when he saw her thousand-kilowatt smile slowly emerge, a smile that made her dark eyes crinkle up at the corners, their color now of sweet hot cocoa on a cold winter day. The punch to his solar plexus didn't hit, however, until he spotted the dimple. Eileen's dimple. He choked on his own breath. Everyone and everything in the room faded into the corners.

"I'm so glad," she said, "that you won't give up."

He barely heard her, could barely remember what they'd been talking about but added, "Me, too." He had to get out of there. "Sara? Sara!"

"Here we are." Sara and Katie converged on him, filling the kitchen to the max. "Hi, Ms. Rebecca," said Sara. "I didn't see you before. Do you live here now?"

Ms. Rebecca nodded. "Just moving in."

"Good." Sara kissed and hugged Ginger and came away with a face covered in licks. The grey, however, remained seated. "Ooh...Ginger likes you. That's good. We can visit you. We live close by. And if you need any help, I can come on my bike."

The woman fidgeted, and Adam stepped in. "Time to go, kids. How does an afternoon at Neptune Park sound?"

His daughter's eyes sparkled. "Sure." She turned to Rebecca. "I love summer the best. It's always such fun."

As though not to be outdone, Katie looked at Rebecca and added, "This Monday, there's a big parade for Memorial Day. Wanna come? It's important but it's fun, too."

"I-I don't know..."

If they stayed any longer, the woman might have a total meltdown. "C'mon, kiddos. Ms. Rebecca has a lot to do. She's moving in, and we're moving out! Let's go." He motioned for Ginger and was surprised when she remained seated. "Come on, girl."

Slowly the dog rose and walked toward him. Then turned her head toward Rebecca and whined softly. The woman leaned forward, clutching the cane. "Oh, you lovely girl." She ruffled Ginger's neck. "I'll see you another time."

Not too soon, he hoped. Nice lady, but not for him. No lady was for him. Not anymore. Eileen had been the one. His relationship with Lila had taught him that. Another tough life lesson. Being burned twice, no matter the reason, was enough. No need to martyr himself simply for a chance at love.

#

At seven o'clock that evening, Becca pulled into a reserved space in the Lobster Pot's parking lot, Josie at her side. "I still can't figure out how we wound up agreeing to dinner with Mr. Quinn's family," said Josie. "You were so against going out."

"I'm still against it, but the man made my head spin. So, I'll make him happy this once and be done with it," said Becca. "It's been a long day and I'm tired. But I owe him. After tonight, I won't feel obligated anymore." She sighed. "I just don't get him. He's being too nice!"

"Whatever. I'm happy to have a great dinner. I've heard about this restaurant. It's supposed to be excellent."

"Well, his daughters own it, run it, and do a lot of the cooking. If they're like their father..."

Josie burst out laughing and added, "Then it won't be a quiet family meal."

Exactly what Becca feared. She'd come to Pilgrim Cove in hopes of a quiet life focused on recovery and planning for the future. Not to be out and about, the center of attention. Tomorrow would be better. She and Josie would stock up her fridge, figure out any overlooked household details, and she'd start her exercises now that her mat was perfectly positioned on a bed in what would become her home therapy room.

She adjusted her seat and got out of the car. "I hate the whole idea of using a handicapped spot. I could walk farther than this." She pointed to the entrance of the place, taking in the wide wraparound porch, tables set outside in the warmer weather.

She felt Josie's arm around her, squeezing gently.

"It's the car door, honey. You need a wide space to open it. You know that. And you can't guarantee you'll have enough space in a regular spot."

Of course Becca knew. "I'm sorry, Jo. Just feeling sorry for myself again."

They walked up two shallow steps to the porch and opened the door to the restaurant. The aromas wafting through the foyer made Becca's salivary glands work overtime. "I'm starving!"

"That's what we like to hear." A blonde woman held out her hand. "Hi there. I'm Maggie Sullivan, partner in the Lobster Pot."

"Then you're Bart Quinn's daughter?" asked Becca.

"That, too," she said with a laugh. "I'm also Lila's mom and Katie's grandma. Come on in. We've been expecting you. Just follow me."

The same high energy as her dad. Another extrovert who'd never met a stranger. But she led them at a moderate pace, and Becca took in everything quickly. The restaurant boasted three separate dining areas all accessed from the center aisle. Maggie led them to the largest area, the main dining room, and to the horseshoe arrangement of tables in the center of the room.

"Thought you'd be most comfortable at the end," said Maggie, leading Becca and Josie to several empty chairs waiting there.

Becca nodded, looked at the two dozen people in the party, and inwardly groaned. Pasting on a smile, she said, "You should have worn name tags. I'll never pass the test."

"'Atta girl," boomed Bart, coming toward her but glancing at the crowd. "Didn't I tell you Sea View House has another winner?"

She recognized a few of them. The pregnant Lila, Doc Rosen, electrician Ralph Bigelow, and Police Chief Rick O'Brien. But now they all had spouses with them. Another ROMEO introduced himself as Sam Parker, only semi-retired. He still worked at Parker Plumbing and Hardware with his older son, Matt. His younger son, Jason, was husband to Lila.

Becca knew she wouldn't remember it all. Didn't want to try. But Sam Parker waved at his family on the other side of the horseshoe. "That's Matt and his wife, Laura." His eyes radiated happiness. "Laura stayed at Sea View House, too, after losing her mom and coping with breast cancer. Then she met Matt and never left Pilgrim Cove. His boys adore her. And they're not alone. I adore her, too!"

"Happy to meet you." But a shiver passed through Becca as she pictured the big house she now occupied. Magic had nothing to do with Matt and Laura. Just simple logistics.

She glanced around the wood-paneled room with the nautical décor. Then she took a closer look at some of the framed posters. One showed a chubby baby in a blue-and-white sailor suit facing the audience. Underneath, the caption read: "It's a buoy!" Down the wall from that one were two young teens in a row boat. "Wouldn't you rudder be fishing?"

"I don't know whether to laugh or groan," said Josie.

"Better laugh," whispered Bart so everyone could hear. "My daughters created those…and you want a great meal tonight!"

She couldn't argue that one. Until she saw Katie and Sara heading her way with Tall, Hazel, and

Handsome in tow. And the only empty seats at the table were next to her and Josie. Her appetite waned.

But it seemed Sara's dad didn't intend to stay. In fact, he barely acknowledged them. "Katie insisted on coming," he apologized to Bart. Then, lowering his voice, he added, "She seems worried about her mother." Adam and Katie continued walking toward Katie's parents. Sara, however, lingered with Becca.

"Katie's going to have a *real* sister," she stated. It wasn't her words that tore Becca's heart but the longing in her voice, the sadness in her eyes…showing the empty space in her life that she was too young to describe. A space with no words.

"I thought you and Katie were sisters the minute I met you," said Becca. "Two beautiful sisters who love each other and Papa Bart."

"Really?" Her eyes widened.

"You girls are like me and Josie. We're sisters in our hearts."

Josie nodded. "That's exactly right."

Sara's smile transformed her from worried to hopeful. "So are Katie and me! We even had a sister ceremony on the beach last year. Right, Daddy?"

Becca hadn't noticed Adam's return. But his daughter probably had sonar sensors in her body to detect the whereabouts of her only parent.

"You sure did, right behind Sea View House."

Sara leaned toward Rebecca. "But no blood," she whispered. "Just a ceremony. We said that 'we're friends forever, filled with love.'"

"It sounds perfect. In fact, here comes Katie again."

The little blonde girl skipped over. "I'm going to sleep at my own house tonight. Just in case my sister gets born."

"But we're sisters, too, Katie. Right?"

"Sure. It's just different…I think. My little sister will have the same mommy and daddy as me."

Sara stared at her hands. Her mouth quivered; her chin trembled. Katie's facts couldn't be refuted.

"Josie and I don't have the same mother and father," Becca said. "And it doesn't matter…"

"Oh, yes it does…" Tears ran down Sara's face. Her shoulders shook. Her dad lifted her, cuddling her close.

"It's okay, baby. I love you. Everyone loves you."

She clung for a second, then wriggled out of his arms. "I know. But you're my dad. You hafta love me. And you know what else? I don't care about Katie and her baby sister! I don't need them. I'm keeping Ginger, and I have all the other beautiful racers and…and all the rescue dogs that need me. That's like having a lot of sisters and brothers."

And if that rationale didn't make lemonade out of lemons, Becca didn't know what could. The child was fighting back with a ten-year-old's logic and passion. Becca glanced at Adam and gasped. The pain— Oh, the pain on his face as he stared at his daughter…

She pressed her lips together. Not her business.

#

"I think you've lucked out, Becca. These people are friendly and warm. Now I won't feel so guilty leaving you on your own when I go back to Beantown on Monday."

Becca started the car and glanced at her cousin. "No guilt, please! Your job is to find us a new place to live by the time the summer's over…unless you and Nick made other plans…?"

The color in Josie's cheeks deepened. "Not yet. I don't think so. We'll see…"

Becca chuckled. "Nice that you know your own mind. Nick's a great guy."

"He is…and I think Adam Fielding has a lot of potential, too. He's a good dad. A very good dad. Too bad he didn't stay for dinner. Poor man has his hands full."

"Everyone has problems." Becca stared straight ahead, focusing on getting back to Sea View House, not wanting to acknowledge the truth of Josie's words, not wanting to think about the vet and his little girl. "I'm realizing that living in a small town like this has major drawbacks."

"Such as…?"

"Such as, everyone knows your business." She bit her lip. By tomorrow, all of Pilgrim Cove would know about her being a victim of the marathon bombing. Even Adam Fielding would find out sooner or later. Despite their support and well wishes, her dinner companions would probably spread the word. And it would pass through town in no time.

"Remember the road sign we saw just as we drove in?" asked Becca.

"Sure do. I laughed so hard, how could I forget?" Josie made quote marks with her fingers. "Population: Winter—5000; Summer—Lots higher."

"I thought it was funny then, too, but I'm not feeling that way now."

"I'm fine with it. Truthfully, Becca, I'm glad they'll all mind your business. I really worry about leaving you alone."

"Get rid of the worry. Get rid of the guilt! I'll be fine."

"It's hard, Becca, when everyone in the rehab center thought you were nuts to come down here by yourself. And not only staff but patients as well. I thought you'd all bonded together and…and listened to each other."

Becca pulled into the Sea View House driveway and shut off the motor. The light from the porch roof shone on Josie's worried face. "We did bond. I made a lot of new friends—wonderful friends—but now just about everyone's gone back to their own homes."

If she closed her eyes, she could picture each one of her new friends learning to adjust to a "different normal." That's how they put it. The multiple wounds, hearing losses, burns, brain injuries, nerve and vascular damage… She'd understood the medical issues more quickly than most of the others. Some, like her, had undergone major or multiple surgeries. They worried about walking again and keeping their jobs. How could she not think about her brave pals and wonder how they were doing?

"The Boston Marathon's a big deal," Becca said. "Lots of people come from out of town. Lots of my new friends live elsewhere. But we email and text. We're keeping up with each other. We're our own support group."

Leaving the rehab center had been hard, though. Mashed up feelings had flowed through her, from happy to scared to excited to worried. And that had been only…what? Two days ago? She patted Josie's arm. "Thanks, cuz."

"For what? I wish I could stay."

"I'm just one of the 265 who were injured. If the other 264 can manage, so can I." She had to relieve Josie's unease. Her loyal cousin deserved a lighter heart. "Just be my eyes and ears at the hospital…I need a job!"

"But you might get some other money, some money from that charity fund."

"Oh, please, Josie. I can't depend on that. Just because I filled out a paper doesn't mean it will amount to anything."

Josie sighed. "I will haunt Human Resources," she said. "I promise."

Becca grinned. "'Atta girl." However, her hopes weren't high. She'd be considered disabled now, and even though accommodations might be made, she couldn't race through the hospital hallways anymore. She wasn't a sitting-down, paper-pushing type. She was an active, hands-on type. A respiratory therapist who worked with patients, teaching them to use equipment, helping them breathe, calming them down. Lately she'd been scheduling staff and supervising them, too. She wanted her career back.

She opened the car door and pivoted in her seat, ready to exit the vehicle.

"And in return," said Josie, "for the house and job hunting I will do, you'll allow me to ask Dr. Fielding to check up on you."

The vet? Her neighbor? "What! Why? Don't you dare…"

"I liked him. And his place is so close. Geez, Bec, he can pop in and say hi when he walks that dog of his. Not even out of his way, so it won't be a problem."

Why didn't Josie understand? Heat rushed through Becca's body; her heart pounded. An explosion of temper should have followed, but Becca's voice reflected none of her internal churning. It came out quiet and cold. In control.

"But it's a problem for me, Josie. I may have lost a leg, but I'm still Becca. If you can't accept my need for independence, then forget about finding a new apartment. Forget the hospital. I'll deal with it. I'll deal with everything by myself."

#

Five minutes later, after Josie had called her an ass and disappeared into her own room, Becca was alone in hers, dealing with her new getting-ready-for-bed activities. Fatigue had set in as soon as she'd closed the door of Sea View House behind her. It wasn't very late, not yet ten o'clock. In the old days, Saturday night would have just begun. She sighed. That was then…this was…

Now consisted of organizing herself. Washing her face and brushing teeth came first. Then she retrieved her crutches, leaned them against the bed, and dug out her pj's. She quickly changed tops, unzipped her slacks and pulled them down. Sitting on the bed, she removed the artificial leg. She was getting used to seeing it now. Made of a lightweight carbon fiber compound, the main pylon wasn't beautiful, but it did the job. The knee mimicked a natural motion thanks to hydraulics, and the foot had been molded to her shape and size. At least her shoes matched. High heels…another matter.

She checked carefully for skin abrasions on her residual limb and automatically applied aloe vera ointment as she'd been told to do. Each square inch of skin contained over six hundred sweat glands and sixty-five hair follicles; she took the directive seriously. An easy enough task to prevent infection and irritation problems. So far, so good since the surgery, including that night. Her skin was clear and healthy. In the morning, she'd select moisturizers and ointments to use before donning the leg. A thick layer of protection every day was mandatory.

Maybe she'd get the hang of these routines in a little while, but now she had to think, plan, and figure everything out. Shortie pajamas wouldn't get tangled with a crutch, so she wore them. She'd need a laundry basket…on wheels…to move her dirty clothes from the bedroom to the machines. Or maybe she could use the wheelchair to transport the laundry bag. The little things might take her down.

Yawning, she scooted under the blanket and made an effort to relax. Only then, through the open window, did she hear the soft whoosh of the ocean washing ashore. A lullaby of the waves. Over and over in an age-old rhythm that could soothe a newborn baby as well as a young woman facing a brand new life.

I hope little Sara hears it, too.

CHAPTER THREE

Becca pushed her shopping cart in front of her, delighted to be perusing the supermarket aisles just like anyone else, walking slowly, making selections. Her cane lay folded in the seat section next to her purse. The cart provided perfect support. And for a moment, for just a brief moment, she felt physically perfect, too. The old normal.

"Food shopping is now my favorite activity. A no-brainer."

Josie's ringing cell phone was the only response. Glancing at the readout, her cousin's eyes narrowed, her nose wrinkled. "Damn. It's the hospital. I'll take it outside, but you're doing great. I'm sure you'll be fine without me for a second." She put the phone to her ear and raced away. Becca shrugged and continued strolling among the fruits and veggies, confident in her skills and in herself.

"Hi, Ms. Rebecca! We're shopping, too." Sara's friendly wave released the child's wagon, which slammed right into Becca's. Thrown off balance, Becca rocked, then grasped the handle tightly enough to turn her fingertips white. Sweat sprouted on her skin. But she remained standing, leaning forward, catching her breath—and at a loss for words.

"Sara! Be careful." Adam Fielding had no such problem and, with one glance at Becca, was at her side, his arm around her. "Are you all right? Can you remain standing? Or would you rather sit down?"

She leaned against him for a moment, recovered her balance, and stood erect again, once more on her own two feet. His arm dropped away, but she sensed him examining her. He took her hand, and his fingers pressed gently against her wrist while he checked his watch.

She took a deep breath. "I'm fine. I'm fine." Ignoring her, he continued in doctor mode. She may have been the wrong species for him, but he knew exactly where to find her pulse, and surprisingly, his touch calmed her. Her breathing slowed to normal.

"Good job," he said with admiration. "Perfect. You handled that really well. My daughter, on the other hand, will be making amends."

Aware of her surroundings again, Becca heard Sara's sobs and apologies. She glanced at the unhappy child, a girl who'd already had a rough couple of days. "Hey, Sara. I'm fine. You didn't hurt me. You just went a little too fast. But you won't do that anymore."

Sara shook her head. "No," she whispered. "Never again."

"Come here, sweetie. You need a tissue, and I've got one." Becca put her hand on Adam's bare arm to regain his attention. His muscle flexed immediately, and she felt the strength that resided there. Strength that she envied. "She's apologized, so don't punish her. No harm done."

Adam swallowed a chuckle while trying to ignore the burn. Who knew that such small fingers could toast a man's skin? And as for Sara, if Rebecca had known them better, she'd realize that Sara wrapped him around her little pinky. But a parent's job went beyond unconditional love. He had to teach and prepare his daughter for the real world. To think ahead. He took a step back.

"We'll be in touch. I know Sara will want to make it up to you."

He was about to walk away, give her some privacy, when he saw her cousin making a beeline for them.

"Hi, all," she greeted before a frown settled on her brow as she turned to Becca. "Change of plans. I have to work tomorrow." She sent an impatient glance from Adam to Becca. "What a surprise. The hospital's short staffed. Could it possibly be because of the holiday weekend?" She sighed deeply. "I'm sorry, Becca. You'll have to take me to the ferry tonight."

Rebecca closed her eyes for a moment. Then nodded. "I suppose it was too much to hope for a three-day weekend for you. But it's just one day difference." She waved at the cart. "I'll buy lots of frozen dinners and food for a week. I'll be fine."

Fine? A crazy idea. How would the woman ever manage alone? Adam didn't know her medical history but could tell she was still groping around, figuring out how to adjust to her disability. "Wait a minute," he said. "I thought you'd both be at Sea View House for the summer."

Rebecca's chin jutted upward. "Where'd you get that idea?" Only a shadow in her dark eyes revealed a doubt. It lurked for a moment before being extinguished. This was one strong lady who wasn't afraid to show it.

"Hmm…where did I get that idea?" Adam raised his brows, felt the corner of his mouth twitch upward. Challenges were familiar territory. Rebecca's ways were different from Eileen's soft, gentle manner, but his wife had been strong, too. Steel magnolia strong had she been southern born. Matching wits with her had been exciting; finding common ground even more so.

"Stop laughing!" demanded Rebecca, pulling him from his thoughts. "Josie has to work. We both do. We're not ladies of leisure. Sure, I was a little nervous at first, but now with those ROMEOs around, it'll be a snap." She clicked her fingers for emphasis. "Don't be concerned at all. It's the way I want it."

Did the woman have any idea of the daily challenges she'd face alone? He could check up on her occasionally, but he had no time to babysit.

Extending her hand, she added, "Nice running into you again, Dr. Fielding. Or should I say crashing?"

"My friends call me Adam," he said.

She smiled. Warm, confident, and with that cute dimple.

And he didn't think about Eileen at all. Dimple or not.

#

"Is she dead?" Sara's voice dropped away, her eyes widening to dinner-plate size.

In the fading light of evening, Adam viewed Pilgrim Cove's newest resident, Sara and Ginger on either side of him. On the back porch of Sea View House, Rebecca lay on a chaise lounge, eyes closed, mouth slightly open. A pair of crutches was propped against a nearby chair. A light blanket covered her, and Adam guessed she'd removed the prosthesis.

"She's fine, Sara. See how her chest is rising with each breath?" he whispered. "Ms. Rebecca is just sleeping. I'd guess she's very tired with all the moving and shopping this weekend."

"She's like Sleeping Beauty." Sara spun toward him, her eyes alight. "You know what, Daddy? You can be the prince. Just one kiss—"

"Oh, no." He knew where Sara would go with this. "Fuggedaboutit, baby. The only princess I see around here is you! So here's your kiss." He lifted his sweet, slender bundle and bestowed a dozen kisses on her neck and cheek. Sara squealed, and a chuckle came from the chaise.

"She's a cutie, but maybe I should install a motion detector around the yard." Rebecca adjusted the chair to a sitting position while trying to stave off Ginger's kisses. The dog had definitely taken a liking to her.

"You're safe enough. A motion detector isn't necessary," said Adam. "We detoured here only because Sara's brought you a gift. She made it herself." His daughter's artistic talent, impressive at ten years old, came straight from her mom. Not only with drawing but in the crafts area, too. "Sara?"

Sara reached into a shopping bag, retrieved the item, and handed it to Rebecca. "It's a treasure box."

Rebecca handled the gift carefully. "Wow! So gorgeous. Look at all those shells…and your designs…beautiful arrangements. Did you really make this?"

"Yup. Katie and I made them for our sister ceremony, too. We put only very important things in the treasure box. Like pictures. And a poem. And anything we love. My mom's picture is in mine. So is Butterscotch's."

"Our cat," explained Adam. "Sara got the short end of that box exchange," he continued. "Katie's talents lie in music, not art."

"Everyone has talent for something," said Rebecca. "I'm a runner." She looked toward the beach, then patted the greyhound. "Just like you, girl. Wanna race?" She hoisted herself from the chair and promptly lost her balance.

Adam caught her in a heartbeat, but his own heart raced faster than a greyhound. "Rebecca! What are you doing?" he shouted, holding her closely and helping her stand. She shivered uncontrollably, but in the mild evening air, he knew it wasn't from cold.

"I forgot! I forgot!" she cried, the shock and despair in her voice echoing into the night.

Forgot? How was that possible? Phantom pain was common, and he could understand that. But she obviously had no pain. He held her close, securely. A lovely package. No doubt about her being a woman. "It's okay," he shushed. "You're all right."

"I was so comfortable and sleeping so well...like it never happened. Such a wonderful feeling. And then I woke up." She closed her eyes. "Why couldn't the dream be real?" she whispered, her question tearing a corner of his heart. "Oh, my God. Could you please hand me the crutches?"

"Only if you don't run into the house." He held his breath, waiting for the explosion.

She turned slightly in his arms and glared at him. How much could he push her? He didn't know her well. But he admired her and didn't want her to fail. Nor did he want to let her go.

#

Of course she wanted to run and hide! She wanted to be alone to cope with her new reality again. She needed privacy. "Crutch, please."

Becca heard him sigh as he held one out to her. Too bad if he was disappointed. She didn't have to please him.

"Coward."

Softly spoken, but she heard him. He still held her close. "Who made you boss?" Her words hissed but matched his low volume.

He nodded toward Sara and Ginger, both sitting at attention, staring at the two adults. "What would you like them to think?"

"Dogs can't think." But the child…? Definitely yes. Little Sara's mind hadn't paused since Rebecca had met her. Adam handed over the second crutch. She grasped it and stepped to the side.

"Dogs can learn," said Adam, "and they can sense things that we can't. Right now Ginger's torn between staying with Sara and going to you." He snapped his fingers for the dog, and she came over immediately, nuzzling Becca before sitting on the ground next to her, simply waiting.

Becca leaned toward the canine, but her hands remained on her crutches. "One day, pretty girl, you and I are going to run on that beach right along the waterline. On the hard-packed sand. We're going to run until we hit twenty-six miles, a true marathon. And we'll do it together."

She received a wet doggie kiss before Adam spoke. "Ginger will leave you in the dust for the first mile. But you'll be twenty-five ahead of her when you reach the finish line."

He tilted his head to the side and stared at her. "All right," he drawled, "I think I get it now. You must have been in Boston two months ago, at the marathon. But you didn't run that day. The runners weren't hurt."

She grabbed the arm of a chair and sat down. "I'd run the marathon in previous years, and I trained hard this year, too. But I was sick that day, running a temp. Did you really not know I was there?"

He shook his head. "What I do know is that you're Boston Strong. You'll run again. One way or another, you'll make it up Heartbreak Hill and get back to the race."

From his mouth to God's ears. Her mother's favorite prayer, short and practical. Adam, however, had voiced her own ardent hope. Another marathon. He'd sounded sincere, had no reason to lie, but he was probably the only person in town who didn't know her story.

"Bart Quinn must have messed up," Becca said. "I thought his megaphone reached everyone."

Adam paused, eyes narrowed, as though reviewing his history with the old man. "Sometimes, he spreads his news selectively."

"I didn't give the guy enough credit," said Becca.

Her cell rang. She reached into her pocket and checked the readout. "Speaking of the devil.... Hi, Mr. Quinn."

She listened. "Well, congratulations, great-grandpa. Rosemary, you say? Nice name. After your wife." Glancing at Adam, she mouthed, *baby born today*. "It's all right. Please don't worry about tomorrow. I don't mind missing the parade. And no, don't call Dr. Fielding to be your stand-in. It's actually not necessary." She sighed and handed the phone to Adam. "He was going to track you down, so you might as well talk to him now."

Adam did more listening than talking before hanging up and speaking to Becca. "Whatever Quinn may think, I'm not his lieutenant, so it's totally up to you. Sara and I usually watch the parade. The whole town shows up. Bart can't get here early enough to take you, but he's reserved a seat for you in the viewing stand at the courthouse. Front and center. He wants to introduce you to the crowd."

"Introduce me?" repeated Becca. "Oh, no, he's not! All I wanted was a quiet summer, a quiet life. But Mr. Quinn doesn't know the meaning of the word."

"I'm going with Daddy," said Sara, breaking into the conversation. "And I'm taking Ginger. Katie has her own real sister now and probably won't even show up. But I like parades!"

Adam glanced down at Becca. "Forget about Quinn. The invitation's wide open and totally your call. Want to make it a foursome?"

Becca looked at each member of the Fielding family one at a time. A dad. A child. A retired racer. All trying to adjust to change. To a new life. Just as she was.

She could feel Adam waiting for her response. Giving her space but perhaps hoping she'd join them. Not that he was hitting on her. Not at all. Tall, Hazel, and Handsome was trying to do the right thing and be neighborly. Maybe preserve the town's reputation? Well, if he made the effort, so could she.

"What time should I be ready?"

#

By nine the next morning, they'd walked two blocks to Main Street and a block north, close to the viewing stand near the courthouse. Not that Rebecca had any intention of sitting with the bigwigs, but seeing and hearing the guest speakers would be nice.

"This is my first small-town celebration of anything," she said. "I've been in Boston for a long time and don't remember attending any event like this when I was a kid." Her mom probably had had no time or interest.

Adam laughed, deep and mellow. A man's voice. "If it's quintessential Americana you're looking for, you've come to the right place." He opened a lightweight folding lawn chair. "Here you go. We'll see everything from this spot. And there's one for Sara, too."

"I'm not tired, Daddy."

42

"Okay. So I'll sit next to Ms. Rebecca. And you...can sit on my lap." He scooped the child up and plopped her on his thighs. Ginger sat herself between the chairs. Within moments, they were surrounded by a small crowd who greeted Adam and Sara with enthusiasm and who were eager to meet the new woman in town. Sara bounded from Adam's lap to play with the dogs many of the residents had brought to the parade. Adam introduced Becca as a summer visitor, now living at Sea View House.

"Welcome to Pilgrim Cove, Rebecca." The petite blonde glanced at the retired police chief. "Sea View House? Did you hear that, Rick? Isn't that great? Did Bart tell you?" The woman threw questions as though they were confetti. She had to be fifty-ish but had the energy of a kid. She turned to her companion, expecting answers.

Instead, Rick O'Brien extended his hand to Rebecca. "Morning, Rebecca. Good to see you again. This is my wife, Dee, who used to manage the diner up the street. Now she's trying to manage Pilgrim Cove!" The teasing light in his eyes removed any trace of criticism his words might have introduced.

"I'm glad you're here," the chief continued, "because last time I was at Sea View House, I forgot to give you this special business card." He pulled one from his shirt pocket and handed it to Becca. "Now you'll know how to find us if you need anything...and nothing's too small. We want you to know right away that you're not alone here. You have friends."

Becca glanced at the card. On the front, in bright red ink, was the word ROMEOs. On the back was a list of eight men—Quinn's name first—along with their phone numbers and skills in bright blue. The down-the-rabbit-hole feeling came over her again. ROMEOs?

More like Quinn's pack of elves. These retirees didn't act retired at all. Business cards?

"Thanks," she said, inserting it into her fanny pack. "I hope I never need it."

"If it gets too quiet, we're good company, too." The chief beamed and turned to Adam. "Still planning that clinic expansion you were working on? Those dogs are lucky to have you in their corner."

"Still planning. But hope to start very soon. I'm waiting to hear about the funding." The couple patted Ginger and greeted Sara before continuing their stroll through the growing crowd.

"Now, about Pilgrim Cove," began Adam, a chuckle lacing his voice. "On the plus side, everyone watches out for everyone else. On the minus side, everyone knows your business."

Becca laughed, too. "I kind of got that. So it's both good and bad."

"You bet." He paused. "I moved here after my wife…after Eileen died. I needed a change of scenery. I brought Sara here for a couple of weeks on the beach during that first summer and decided to stay."

"That was a big decision. Are you ever sorry?"

He took another moment to consider. "No. She's happy here. Safe. Secure. This little dust-up with Katie will pass, and she's got other friends, too."

Sara's well-being was the key to his. Becca understood that immediately. Adam didn't say anything about his own happiness, about *him* being happy in Pilgrim Cove. It was all about his daughter.

"She's lucky to have you." Just like Chief O'Brien had said about the greyhounds' good luck. Seemed like Adam Fielding filled a lot of needs around here. Perhaps he simply liked to be needed.

"I try to be a good dad," he said, "but…" He shrugged.

But he thought he fell short. If he only knew... "Every parent thinks they do things wrong whether they're single or part of a couple." With one exception. Becca doubted her own mother thought about parenting at all. Sure, her mom loved her, but Angela Hart focused only on earning her next dollar, her next month's rent. But would Becca have done any better had positions been reversed?

"And how would you know about parenting?" Adam teased, a slow grin spreading across his face. "Have a dozen kids hidden away somewhere?" His hazel eyes turned a golden hue while a lock of brown hair fell onto his forehead. He pushed it back impatiently.

A fluttering sensation started in Becca's stomach as she watched the serious dad transform into one fine package of manly. Her breath hitched when he smiled at her.

"Maybe someday I'll think about kids..." Rebecca matched Adam's shrug, playing it cool. *Someday*, of course, was a fairy tale. No guy would ever consider a serious relationship with her. Logic had forced her to accept the facts as soon as she'd understood the consequences of the bombing. But...damn it! At times, anger toward the perpetrators filled her to the point of gasping. How dare they?

But they had dared. And couldn't destroy her. Despite everything, she realized she was still Rebecca! Still a woman. Who wanted to lead a full life when she was ready for it. And if men couldn't see that—if they saw her only as an object of pity—it was their loss. She exhaled deeply, trying to get a grip. The authorities had nabbed the perps, one still alive. So she seemed to strike back at the entire male population. She definitely needed an attitude adjustment, especially with Adam, who'd been totally at ease with her.

"I hear music!" Sara squealed.

"So do I!" agreed Rebecca, glad for the distraction. She craned her neck to view the procession. And there, for the first time in her life, she viewed a small-town parade. Classic Americana. Just as Adam had promised. The grand marshal, a retired Navy commander, headed the procession. Behind him followed several flag bearers. The Boy and Girl Scouts marched, throwing candy to spectators. Sara caught a piece. "Daddy says I should join the Girl Scouts this year."

"Do you want to?" asked Becca.

"But what if I don't have enough time to help with the rescues?"

Becca hugged the child. Couldn't help it. "At least think about it."

"Oh, look! Here comes the marching band. Katie's cousin, Brian, is in it. He's only twelve, but he can play lots of instruments."

"Talented boy. Just like you're a talented girl."

Behind the band and in step with the patriotic songs came the volunteer fire department, proudly displaying their fire trucks. The Little League baseball and softball teams followed on their floats. Sara waved hard at the children. "I play softball, too," said Sara. "But I'd rather watch the whole parade than ride with them."

Sara sure had her preferences.

Traffic had been rerouted to the outermost surrounding streets so the whole town could celebrate together. Becca jumped to her feet. "This is great," she said to Adam. "So impressive. Who knew?"

#

Her excitement emanated from every pore. Her eyes sparkled; a pink blush covered her cheeks. No doubt Rebecca Hart was a beautiful woman—who might have fallen on her head if he hadn't caught her. Again.

"Easy does it."

She regained her balance fast. "I keep forgetting…" she admitted, her complexion flaming. "When I'm distracted…you know, caught up in *real* life, the rest of it fades away."

"Like that's not real?" he asked, nodding toward her leg.

Her chin lifted, she met his stare. "It's real, but it doesn't define who I am. I won't let it. I've been hurt, but I'm not dead!"

Dead? He'd never seen anyone so alive, and he might have told her except that a familiar voice came over the speaker system. Bart Quinn was at the mic.

"A day of reflection," he began, "a chance to say thank you to the men and women who have fought or are currently fighting for our freedom."

He introduced the grand marshal, who took over the speech making.

"Whew," Adam whispered. "The guy's been known to go on and on…"

Rebecca's grin charmed him. "I'm relieved, too," she replied. "I was afraid he'd put a spotlight on me. I don't trust that oversized leprechaun for a minute…"

As Adam focused his attention on Bart, he saw the man searching the crowd, his eyes stopping when they alighted on him and Rebecca. A grin splashed across the older man's face, followed by a satisfied expression. Adam glanced at Becca. She and Sara looked content together, listening to the speaker, and he hesitated to spoil Rebecca's mood. He remained quiet.

Five minutes later, however, after the Navy commander had stepped down, Adam nudged Becca. "Bart's got the mic again. Prepare yourself."

He watched her look around, probably searching for an escape route. The sidewalks were crowded. Folks were zoned in on the speakers' platform.

"Memorial Day is really about the ones who didn't make it home," said Bart Quinn. "It's also about the ones who are fighting now. And remembering them is our legacy for the next generation...a member of which happens to be my brand new great-granddaughter born yesterday." He grinned and waved at the crowd.

Applause broke out. Cheers. Adam heard Rebecca's chuckles. Saw her shake her head. "He's quite something. Pilgrim Cove's Barnum and Bailey rolled into one."

Bart held up his hands, and the crowd settled down. "I had to mention the lassie because this is also a celebration of our town. And the wee Rosemary is its newest citizen. Sweet and innocent. We all start out that way. But sometimes an innocent citizen becomes a hero whether she wants to or not. We've got one of those in Pilgrim Cove right now, too. She didn't know it two months ago on Patriot's Day. She didn't know she'd become a hero at the finish line in Boston. She didn't know then that she'd become a victim of war simply by watching a race. But she's wicked strong, is Rebecca Hart."

From flaming red to stark white. If Becca's complexion got any paler, she'd pass out. "Want to leave?"

"I wasn't a hero!" she spat. "I was just in the wrong place at the wrong time. Let's get out of here."

"Yes, ma'am." Adam took less than ten seconds to fold the chairs, grab the leash, and head out between the people surrounding them. "Just follow me," he said, carving a path.

"I'll-I'll try."

He snapped his head around to check on her. Rebecca was several feet behind him.

"God almighty! I want to fly, but I can't even run," said Rebecca.

Change tactics. "Then your alternative is to brazen it out. Bart's waving at you right now."

"I'll kill him."

"Just wave back and smile. Pretend."

#

So she did. She didn't have much choice. Taking Adam's advice, she made believe she was Meryl Streep or Sandra Bullock. Of course, she'd never shared those women's dreams of acting. Of performing in front of millions. The spotlight was not for her. Bart's voice, however, still boomed through the air.

"Our heroine, Rebecca Hart, also a victim of war, will be staying with us for the summer at Sea View House. Stop by there and visit. With no relatives in town, she could use some new friends."

The man was crazy. Entertain friends? Crowds? She must have been out of her mind to come to this town by herself. The mass of humanity around her now was…was just too much. She was in the center of a whirlwind. Choking. As though perched on a cloud, she looked down at the colorful gathering and saw herself, a clone of Rebecca Hart. She wondered how she got there. Or was she zoning out? People talked about out-of-body experiences. Was she experiencing one?

"I-I have to leave. Really, really, I have to get out of here. I need to be alone." Several blocks of walking awaited her. Speed walking, if she had her way.

Adam's arm settled around her. A familiar touch now, and she relaxed. His steady directives to Sara reassured, as well. "Take Ginger and walk ahead of us to the corner. Hold her leash tightly with two hands and be alert. You know the drill. Wait until we get there."

They walked toward Sea View House at a safe, steady pace under a bright sun. No one spoke until

Rebecca broke the silence. "I feel fine. So maybe I'm the crazy one."

She tilted her head back and looked up at Adam Fielding, a man she'd met two days ago in a bar and who'd stared at her with dislike. A man who'd just rescued her from public speaking. A man she was beginning to trust. But a man who'd just glimpsed her fear. Her panic. Sure, he'd done the honorable thing, but he probably couldn't wait to get rid of her at Sea View House. Drop her off and leave.

"Thank you."

His brows shot up. "For what? You've gone through hell, still going through the aftermath, and you've got nothing to prove to anyone. Including Quinn. In fact, including me."

Of course she had something to prove. If he thought they were on a level playing field, he was wearing rose-colored glasses. She couldn't even hold a job yet.

He looked around them as they walked, perhaps checking for eavesdroppers. "Some people prefer quieter lives...and more privacy than others. Bart Quinn's never met a stranger. He and his family are not only extroverts but I'd call them extreme extroverts, absorbing energy from the people and the air around them. They're great folks, but most folks aren't like that."

"I think I agree." She peered up at him. "Are you including yourself in the quieter group?"

His friendly smile touched her. "I know myself pretty well," he offered. "Sara and I lead a pretty routine life between school and work. People trust me with their animals, and my practice is doing well. I'm also trying to expand the rescue work I do." His loving gaze rested on his daughter. "We've both made enough friends not to be bored. Sara's happy so I'm happy. Both our lives are jam-packed, and we're satisfied just as we are."

He may have worded it kindly, but his message to her came through loud and clear. His docket was full to capacity. No room for anyone else.

CHAPTER FOUR

The first phone call that afternoon came from Bart Quinn. The man almost apologized for putting her on the spot. With so many "lassies" peppering his speech, she wound up swallowing a few giggles. No doubt about it. The good-hearted curmudgeon had been blessed with the gift of gab.

The second call came from her mother, who'd be visiting for a few days two weeks down the road. Good. Becca could handle her mother. Maybe help Angela adjust to the new reality in their family. The new Rebecca.

Her surprising disappointment about Adam, however, took up most of her thoughts. She hardened herself bit by bit as she performed her series of tough exercises on her mat. She ignored the sweat and strain as she faithfully kept going, one stretch, one lift, one resistance move after another. Building muscle, not only in her residual limb but in her entire body, was imperative. Independence required strength. With strength, she could conquer the backyard of Sea View

House and get closer to that ocean view...a priceless gift to herself.

When shadows fell and evening arrived, Rebecca left the porch and, without her cane, carefully made her way over the uneven terrain of the grassed yard until she reached the wall of the property. The boards had been removed, and she was able to lower herself to the granite ledge. Inhaling the salty air, she rejoiced in her accomplishment and, immodestly, her can-do attitude. She rejoiced in being closer to the water's edge—grass behind her, sand before her. She rejoiced in being under an open sky.

She watched the sun fade in the west, across town, leaving only a swath of pale orange rays in its wake. As evening emerged, the beach darkened, and the last few sunbathers packed up and made their way home. Tomorrow was a work day for them. But not for Becca. She'd have the pleasure of watching another spectacular sunrise over the ocean. For the first time since leaving the rehab center, being behind in her career worried her less. Her work now, she reminded herself, was to get stronger.

She closed her eyes and inhaled again. The sea air was better than any medicine. From the top of her head to the toes of her foot, she could feel her muscles become as relaxed as unused rubber bands. If this was the magic Quinn was talking about, she'd give him points for it. One more deep breath and she'd fall asleep on the wall!

Several breaths later, she sensed the presence of others but wasn't alarmed. Maybe Bart's baloney about Pilgrim Cove was starting to infuse her. Slowly, she raised her lids. Ginger sat quietly before her, waiting, her leash trailing from her harness. Her attention was focused on Becca as though the playful ocean didn't exist. As though a man and child weren't running toward them across the sand.

"I think you're in trouble, my girl," said Becca, stroking the greyhound on her neck and chest. But Becca was in trouble, too. She hadn't counted on another conversation with Adam, at least not so soon.

Ginger licked Adam and Sara when they joined her. The dog didn't seem to know or care about running away from her people.

"Sorry, Rebecca," said Adam. "She's still learning how to be a family dog. Her instinct is to run when she sees something she wants. Greys are sight hounds, which is why they run track chasing a mechanical rabbit. But they'll chase after anything that moves."

"I was sitting still."

Sara said, "But she loves you already, Ms. Rebecca. She thinks you're her family, too."

That plaintive note again. "I don't agree, sweetie. She knows you and your dad are her family. She might think that I'm her job. That she has to keep me company or something." She beckoned the girl closer. "In the hospital where I worked, volunteers brought their dogs to visit patients. They helped the patients relax and feel better."

"Wow. Maybe Ginger can do that."

"Maybe," replied Becca. "Those dogs had to take classes first and learn how to behave in a hospital."

Sara beamed at her. "Ginger's so smart she won't have to go to school. She just knows how to help you."

Good lord, what had she started?

"Ms. Rebecca is doing quite well," said Adam. "With or without Ginger." He turned to Becca. "I really mean that. It's barely been two months, and your gait is excellent."

"My gait?" she snapped, unconcerned now about another conversation with this man. "I appreciated your help this morning at the parade, Adam, but I'm not your patient. Maybe you're the one who needs a class in manners. Take another look. I've got two legs, not four."

He stepped closer but held his hand up. "Believe me, I've noticed the whole package. I notice a lot. My brain works automatically, and I can't turn it off on a whim. It's the same thing as an optometrist checking out people's glasses at a party, in a supermarket, everywhere." He pivoted toward his daughter. "Sara, honey, we've got to get going. You have school tomorrow."

As Adam gathered his family together, Becca gazed over his shoulder, her last words echoing in her mind over and over again.

"I do have two legs! Two good legs. Which work just fine." If she needed to convince herself, so be it. She waved her arm at the powerful Atlantic and the expanse of sand before it. "And tomorrow, I'm going to walk on that beach. And someday, somehow, I'll get into the water and swim."

Adam glanced toward the shoreline. Only at the water's edge was the sand hard-packed and perhaps possible for Becca to navigate. Maybe. A big maybe. Unexpected dangers could lurk. Hidden air pockets, clumps of seaweed, piles of shells, or a visitor's forgotten item. Between the house and the water, however, he saw bigger trouble. Dry, shifting sand. Irregular and uneven, the kind of surface anyone could struggle with. What she attempted, of course, wasn't really his business, but his mouth had other ideas.

"No. You're not ready."

"Excuse me?"

One look at her outraged expression and he wanted to eat his words. He should have realized that Becca wasn't one to take orders. At least not from him. He'd back off. For now.

"Just stating the obvious, but...what do I know?" He shrugged. "Do what you want. And carry a cell phone. You'll probably need it."

"I've been an athlete all my life. I'm betting on me."

He saw her chin rise, her mouth tighten. He saw her determination as she rose from the rock wall and stood, poised for flight. Like the nightingale in its cage, this beautiful woman yearned for freedom, yearned to fly along the shore. She didn't hide her emotions—didn't try to—and he read them as clearly as if she'd shouted her desires to the world. She'd run marathons once, only a short while ago. How could she now sit and wait?

"Make no mistake, Rebecca. I'm betting on you, too. But not tomorrow." He stepped closer and her chin rose, her eyes resting on him. His hand automatically moved to her cheek, and he stroked the soft skin. As soft as the singing bird's delicate wings. "Your recovery isn't a sprint. It's a marathon, exactly as your races were."

Her eyes remained open, shiny and curious. His thumb trailed over her lips. He stroked them and felt her warm breath as they parted slightly. His heart rate surged. "So approach it the same way," he advised, his voice hoarse. "Little by little. With a lot of training. You'll run again; you'll race again. Just not yet."

Sweet. Strong. A beautiful siren. He leaned in, wove his fingers through her thick hair, and kissed her.

#

She wasn't expecting it. The roar she heard in her ears did not come from the ocean but from the touch of Adam's mouth on hers. The man knew how to kiss. Her hands fluttered to his shoulders, not to push him away but to feel, press, and appreciate his strength. She tasted him and stored the flavor in her memory bank. They hardly knew each other, but she didn't care. Not then. Later, she'd chalk up this insanity to a pale sun, a gentle breeze, and the romantic ambiance of the beach, a moment she'd remember. But now his mouth touched her in a serious way, as a man kisses a woman. A real man and a real woman. It felt right. He seemed not to give a fig about her leg, except for giving too much advice.

"I hadn't planned that... I didn't know..." Adam whispered. "I'm sorry...especially...good God!" He twirled, obviously searching for Sara, who stood statue-still with Ginger at her side. "Especially with my daughter..." He shook his head, murmuring, "Unbelievable. Even with Lila, I never messed up like that."

"I wouldn't worry about it," said Becca as butterfly wings brushed against her heart. "There are worse things a child could witness. I think she'll survive." She caught the tiny grin appearing on Sara's face and grinned back. "She'll definitely survive."

Adam glanced from one female to the other, but his gaze lingered on Becca. "She might survive, but that avoids the real question. Doesn't it?"

She swallowed hard. His words hinted at a growing friendship, perhaps even something more...but...?

"No harm done, Adam. Blame it on—on the moment."

"Then I'm taking another one, Rebecca. And I'm going to kiss you again."

#

She'd given him a way out. So why hadn't he taken it? As he walked to work the next morning, Adam's eyes felt like sandpaper. Lack of sleep could do that to a person. What was it about Rebecca that kept him tossing and turning? He was done with relationships. After heartbreak with Eileen and disappointment with Lila, he'd had enough. Fugeddaboutit! But then came Rebecca with a delicious smile and courage to spare. A thoroughbred who knew her own worth. She had the confidence he wanted Sara to develop. Hadn't Becca shown it in their first encounter at the Wayside Inn when she'd stared him down? He chuckled at the memory. Hard to believe they'd met only four nights ago.

He opened the front door to the clinic, pleased with what he saw—the windowed reception area and general layout—but impatient to begin the expansion.

"Morning, Dr. Fielding." Arlene Farr, his assistant and office manager, greeted him with a smile. She brought not only ten years' experience but a love of animals to the job. She handed him the surgery list for the day. "The patients are all here. Peggy finished the blood work and vitals. Your turn now."

"Thanks." His two-person staff arrived an hour before he did, getting patients ready for their day. The pet parents, too! He couldn't run the place without the two women. After a few mishaps with new hires, he'd wound up with a cohesive and dedicated group—a skilled veterinary technologist and a super-efficient office coordinator. His "office wives."

He riffled through the paperwork and began triaging the cases. The most serious ones went first to give the pets more time to recuperate before going home. His clinic was not an overnight facility, at least not yet. Except for emergencies, most patients went home at the end of their big day.

Becca invaded his thoughts as soon as he left the operating room and headed for lunch. In the break room, reaching for a sandwich, his hand poised over the bread.

"What are you smiling about, Doc?" asked Peggy. "You've got a dozen callbacks, and that waiting room is going to be full in an hour."

He hadn't realized he was smiling. He glanced at Peggy—sharp, perceptive, and bossy at times. Perhaps because she'd grown up with three younger brothers and now had two sons and a husband to boss around, a husband who adored her.

"I'm famished," he said. "And the sandwich looks good."

"I bet that's not the whole story," said Arlene, stretching out her words. "There's a new little gal in his life. I was at the parade. You can't hide in Pilgrim Cove."

Once more, he was reminded of the downside of a small town. But the women were right. "Be nice to her. She's had a rough time."

Arlene and Peggy did that eye roll thing with each other. "Uh-oh. He's on another rescue mission," said Peggy.

"What?"

"You've got a soft heart, Adam. Perfect for a great vet."

"My heart's not involved at all, so get that straight. Just being neighborly." Not exactly true, but true enough for these gals.

The phone rang and Adam retreated to his private office. The ladies had one thing wrong. Becca didn't need rescuing. She could take care of herself—if she used common sense.

During the next hour, he spoke with clients and a pharmacy rep who wanted to do a "lunch and learn" session, and went next door to take Ginger for a short walk.

He thought about calling Rebecca but refrained. She needed space. He got that. Independence was her favorite word. No rescue mission here, but he hoped he'd be first on her list of calls if she needed help. Better yet, if she wanted company.

#

Handle it yourself! You can do this.

Rebecca lay on the kitchen floor, her heart racing. Shock and fear had that effect. One dropped towel, one little misstep, and boom. A fall. Her cell was in her pocket, but dang if she would call anyone. Her therapist at the rehab center had gone over the "how to get up from a fall" part of the survival skills. Falls were inevitable—for other people. She hadn't counted on falling herself. Not with her excellent balance... She sighed. Excellent balance before the marathon.

Lying on her back, she inhaled deeply, then exhaled. She inhaled and exhaled a second time, trying to reestablish her normal rhythm. Trying to calm herself enough to think. Everything had happened so fast, and that was the part no one could really prepare for. The surprise. The speed.

She wasn't hurt and began rolling onto her own right knee, with elbows and hands on the floor, sort of like a sprinter. Three points of support. She grabbed on to a chair seat, thankful for strong arms and hands, glad she'd been faithful to her exercises. She maneuvered herself onto her good knee, then pushed down against the chair until she stood and got her balance. Pivoting, she finally collapsed onto the chair, perspiration dotting her entire body.

"And that's enough physical therapy for today," she murmured to herself.

"Nice job."

Startled, she turned swiftly on the chair and stared at the man who'd been on her mind all night. The man she'd enjoyed kissing and who knew how to kiss. But she wasn't happy to see him.

"Breaking and entering? Don't you know how to knock?"

"I did knock. You were busy."

"I'm still busy. Go away." To her horror, she felt her mouth tremble, her eyes fill. It had to be a delayed reaction to the fall and the thought of what could have happened.

"You handled it perfectly." Adam's calm voice soothed her.

"Perfectly?" She took a deep breath, buried her tears. "I don't know about that. I just did the best I could. But I think I'll pin the dish towel to my jersey from now on." No more falls. No more accidents.

Adam stared at her, at the kitchen sink and counter. "I have an idea, but I've got to get back to the office now. Ginger's outside on your porch, and Sara will be home from school soon. So don't do anything stupid until later. I mean…just don't do anything stupid."

"Stupid? Stupid!" she spewed back. But he was gone, and her question floated only to her own ears.

Had she made a mistake in coming to Sea View House? In living alone? Suddenly, she missed Josie's presence. The comfort of someone she loved and trusted. She missed her mom, too. Despite her jaded outlook on life, Angela Hart had provided a stable home—a roof and a full fridge.

Damnit! Weak moments were for weak people. She got up, grabbed her cane, and went to the door. Then she walked across the yard to the beach.

\#

"Katie said her new sister was kind of boring."

"Oh?" At dinner that evening, Adam put his fork down, curious to see where this conversation was going.

"Yup. All little Rosemary does is sleep and cry and eat."

"Sounds about right, don't you think? You've been around lots of newborn pups and kittens. Do they do more than that?"

"Nope. But Rosemary is a person! Katie says she can't even play with her yet, so she wants to come here after school tomorrow. Just like before."

"If it's okay with her mom and dad, then sure." It seemed like Sara's world was starting to right itself again. He'd known it would, but the relief he felt right now was palpable. "So, are things going back to normal between you and Katie?"

"Dad! Of course they're normal. Katie is my sister in my heart. We'll always be best friends. Don't you know anything?"

Anything? How about nothing? How about he was punting again, like he'd been doing for years now. Were all dads as clueless?

"Homework done?"

He checked her homework as he did every night, proud of her accomplishments and of her ability to learn. He loved seeing her essays on the classroom bulletin board along with her art projects. "Good job, kiddo," he praised as he scanned a math paper.

Sometimes he wondered if he should push her harder, maybe urge the school to let her skip a grade. Her report cards showed all As. On the other hand, she'd always been happy in class with her friends. Fourth grade was no different. Sara's doting grandparents thought she was a genius. "So bright!" his mom always said. "Just look at what she can do." But even he knew to draw a line at "genius." Raising kids was a balancing act. A difficult tightrope walk.

"It's still light outside. Want to go out for a while with me?"

Sara's eyes sparkled. "To see Ms. Rebecca?"

"To see Matt Parker at the hardware store. I need to buy something."

His daughter's eager expression changed to disappointment. "Oh, all right. But let me hold Ginger's leash."

"While I carry the plastic bag for pickup duty?" he joked.

"Yes, sir. Your turn." Her dimple was adorable, and he gave her a quick kiss. "Let's load the dishwasher and go."

Joking was fine, but a yellow caution light started blinking in his mind. Only four days and Rebecca's name drew Sara like a moth to a lit candle. Little girls, he reminded himself, were impressionable. Just as young boys looked to their older brothers and sports heroes as role models, young girls studied teenagers and women. He shuddered at the image of celebrity role models. Girls, he thought ruefully, were more complicated than boys. Physically and emotionally. Especially youngsters without a mother.

When Rebecca left Pilgrim Cove at the end of the summer, Sara might miss her, especially if they became friendlier. He pictured the tears and heartbreak. But wasn't that life? Real life? People came and went all the time. Sighing, he put it out of his mind. No point borrowing trouble. He'd deal with the situation when he had to.

#

Becca was dozing on the chaise in the backyard but knew she had company. She seemed to have developed a sixth sense about Adam and Sara. And Ginger, too. She heard the dog's pant. The little girl's soft, high voice. The man's low pitch.

"Daddy, she's sleeping. Again! She's always sleeping."

Becca's lids flew open. "No, I'm not. I'm just…just…"

"Resting her eyes," said Adam. "She uses a lot of energy—more than we do—during the day."

Becca waved them to sit down. The porch sported a redwood picnic table, benches, and several other chaise lounges. "Could have been worse, but I was a coward."

His brow hitched. "Explain that."

"I walked across the grass to the stone wall again. Didn't even use the cane. All by myself." She gazed ahead at the wall now. "I sat on the wall, shifted around, and stood up on the other side, on the sand."

"Sand? Loose sand? With no support?" he bellowed, making Sara jump. Adam's hazel eyes had darkened. Becca could make out the pulse beating in his neck, sensed his frustration, a slow simmer. So different than his usual upbeat attitude.

"I was disappointed in myself once I took a step and sank in," she said. "Off-balance. Fear hit me. Paralyzed me. I've never been afraid of any fitness challenge in my entire life. And there I was…afraid to put one foot in front of the other and just plain old walk."

"Excellent decision," said Adam. "Common sense is not overrated. It's how we survive." He paused, coughed, and avoided looking at her. "You made a good judgment call. A-one, in fact."

Maybe. But she'd hated it. She'd lost her freedom. Lost a part of herself and the woman she'd once been. She'd never be that woman again. She had to reinvent herself, and the thought unnerved her.

Of course, if she had a million dollars, she'd come close to her former self. With that kind of money, she could buy a unique prosthetic leg for all occasions—general sports, a blade foot for sprinting, a leg for swimming and showering. She'd heard that the aqua limb wasn't very expensive in comparison to the others, especially to the cosmesis limb, which looked exactly like a real leg. Made to match the individual, skin tone, freckles, tattoos, everything. People couldn't tell the difference. And it had feet that could adjust to high-heeled shoes. The cosmesis limb, however, cost a fortune. She emitted a deep sigh. A huge sigh. People called her a hero, but she didn't feel like one.

Adam reached over from the adjacent chaise and squeezed her hand. She didn't pull away. "You never *get over* grief, you just learn to live with it."

Grief...? The word made sense. Despite all her bravado, she was still grieving for her old self, in mourning for the old Rebecca. The thought jostled. Intrigued. She'd never used that word, but he'd nailed it. Adam knew about grief.

"We brought you another present," said Sara. "Daddy, can we give it to her now? All this talk is boring. Even Ginger's yawning."

"Sure we can." He glanced at Rebecca. "It's not the usual gift for a lady."

"That's for sure," added Sara, "but maybe you'll like it anyway. It's from the hardware store. It's...it's practical." She rolled her eyes and handed a box to Rebecca. "Open it."

She did. And stared. Practical was one thing, but...this was a mystery.

"Do you like it?"

Becca looked at Sara's concerned face, the touch of anxiety clearly showing. "I love it! How thoughtful of you." And what the heck was this gift that Adam thought was so wonderful? "Thank you so much." She eyed the girl's father, her meaning unmistakable.

"Take it out of the box, Sara, and Rebecca will see what a great idea this is."

Sara followed directions, and soon a weird-looking apron appeared. "I saw the whole thing stretched out in the store," the girl said. "It goes around your waist and has more pockets than a kangaroo. They're marsupials, you know, and they've got only one pocket."

"It's called a carpenter's apron," Adam added quietly. "Eleven pouches. Various sizes. Made of suede leather so it's strong, too."

She didn't need any further explanation. She could put her comb and brush in one pouch, a pocket mirror, lipstick, tissues, keys, even...a dishtowel in others. And her cell phone. She could put a book or her E-reader in a large pouch. She'd have all the essentials with her at all times in one place. One easy-to-find place.

"This is...is really fantastic," she said, swallowing hard. "It's the most thoughtful gift anyone could have given me. So thank you so much." She turned to Sara. "Come here, sweetie." And she hugged her until she had no breath left.

"My turn?"

She blinked at Sara's dad. His upbeat persona was back in place. "I meant what I said, Adam. It's a wonderful gift. Thank you so much. I'd offer to pay you because I would have bought it myself—if I'd have thought of it. You're amazing. Really amazing."

And that's when his complexion turned ruddy. He whistled for the dog and gathered Sara to him. "It was a guy thing. Any guy would have thought of it."

Her therapists hadn't. Her surgeons hadn't. Only Adam had.

"Thank you again."

"You can thank me by getting up and putting it on. I want to see how it fits and how you walk before I leave."

She rose from her chair, got her balance, and reached for the apron. "I'm really strong, Adam, no matter what you may think. In fact, I've got an appointment in Boston tomorrow at the rehab center."

He looked startled. "How're you getting there? Driving for two hours?"

"Nope. I'm taking the ferry. It'll be an adventure."

"A walk on the wild side, eh? Well, call me when you get back."

She opened the kitchen door and stood on the threshold. "Sure. Sure. I'll call. Hmm…what's your number?" She handed him the ROMEOs' business card. "Just add it to the list."

He glanced at it quickly. "Oh, my creaking bones. I'm not eligible."

She giggled, glad he found the humor of it. "Let's call it the list of *important* numbers."

"Then mine goes first. Above Bart Quinn's."

#

Becca parked her car at the Pilgrim Cove harbor and made her way to the ferry dock. She wasn't alone. Doc Rosen and his wife, Marsha, along with Sam Parker were headed to an afternoon concert of the Boston Pops. A sunny day for congregating outside on the open deck. The water was calm, and Becca chose to stand at the railing and feel the wind on her face. She'd sit down on the return trip, after her therapy.

The seniors greeted her like a long-lost daughter. They beamed at her love of Sea View House. "Worth every penny I'm not paying just for the backyard," she said. "I am so lucky to have found it." Fact was fact.

"Oh, sure. The sliding scale," said Doc. "No one knows what anyone pays. That is one thing our fearless leader keeps to himself, and you don't have to explain."

"I know. I'm just not used to that kind of thing…"

"One day, you'll pass the favor to someone else. That's the way it works." Marsha Rosen spoke. "You've got a long life ahead of you, Rebecca. Opportunities knock all the time. And by the way, your cute fanny pack is a great idea. Denim works with everything."

Becca laughed. "If you like this little one, you should see the one I got last night from Adam and Sara." As she described her kangaroo apron, she saw eye contact among the three others. Suppressed smiles as well.

"He's a good man, that Adam Fielding," said Sam Parker. "Almost married my daughter-in-law, Lila, but then Jason came home. First love reunited, mistakes forgiven, and now a new baby. I guess it's true that love conquers all."

Adam had had a first love, too. His Eileen. The ending, of course, was different, but the emotions… ? Maybe they carried on.

"Adam made an excellent choice with that apron. Very thoughtful, extremely thoughtful," said Doc. He stepped closer, his eyes enlarged behind his wire-framed glasses. "Like Sam said, Adam Fielding's a good man. And you're living in Sea View House. Just think about it."

Her new friends couldn't have made more pointed statements if they'd broadcasted over a speaker system. But they were so cute, trying to plant their seeds for a love story.

"He's medically trained," said Becca. "The choice of gift was just a 'guy thing.' His words. A neighborly thing to do." She smiled. "I've got other items on my agenda now."

"And you'll let us know how you make out today," said Doc Rosen. "I want to keep an eye on you."

Sweet. The doc was sincere. He took his ROMEO responsibility seriously. No matter, it still felt good to hear his request. "I wouldn't have believed it last week," said Rebecca, "but I'm glad to have met you, to have so many people in my corner here. Like a Pilgrim Cove team."

"My dear," began Marsha Rosen, "no one remains a stranger for long in this town. Whether it's a sojourner at Sea View House or a new resident who buys outright. When you're only a 'finger in the ocean,' as Bart likes to say about us, everyone gets to know each other."

Mrs. Rosen's innocent explanation caught Becca by surprise. She'd been so concerned about her privacy and living behind her own walls, she'd forgotten she liked to socialize. She had lots of friends in Boston—from school and work. She had friends she'd grown up with in her hometown. She'd sent them all away after the bombing, and they'd respected her wishes.

This easygoing conversation with her new neighbors, however, felt right. Maybe it was time to send her friends a different signal and hope they'd respond. Another step forward to her new normal.

CHAPTER FIVE

She dragged herself home. No doubt about being tuckered out. Exhausted. Disappointed, too. She shouldn't have been surprised about it after a full day with aggressive therapists followed by a visit to the prosthetist's office to adjust the fitting of her leg in addition to the traveling back and forth. She'd considered herself hardier than that, however, and was surprised and disappointed in her flagging stamina. It seemed the more exercise she did, the more challenges the staff gave her. At the end of the day, however, her entire team had been pleased. She could exercise in Pilgrim Cove for the next two weeks as long as no complications arose.

Sitting quietly on the return ferry that evening, Becca looked forward to arriving at Sea View House and relaxing behind its stout walls. She'd get into her pj's, read a book or watch a sitcom on television. She'd earned a lazy evening. In addition to her aerobics and strength training, perhaps the move to Pilgrim Cove had depleted more energy—both physical and emotional— than she'd realized. She'd narrow her focus in the future, be less distracted by her new surroundings. And by new people. Her transitional life in Pilgrim Cove was exactly that. Transitional. Until she found a new home.

Tomorrow afternoon she'd begin mixing strength training with cardio at the outpatient P.T. center in Pilgrim Cove's medical clinic. She'd already scheduled the appointment, and now she could update the type of exercise she needed to do. Despite all her progress to date, she still had goals to meet. Her recovery required pacing, strategy, and good health.

She entered Sea View House just as her cell rang. One glance at the readout and she smiled. Adam. "Hi," she said. "I just walked through the door."

"Good. I've got a question for you. How'd you like to walk through my door early tomorrow morning and go to work? My office manager had a family emergency and will be out of town for a couple of weeks. Want a temporary job?"

Did money grow on trees? Of course she did. She squeezed the receiver and listened to Adam's continuing spiel. He was still trying to sell her.

"It's simple," he said. "Meet and greet, answer phones, schedule appointments, sterilize instruments. More important, talk to the pets...and don't forget their owners."

She heard the smile in his voice, loved the sound of his accompanying laugh. Low. Musical. Upbeat.

"I can handle patients, at least human ones, but I've got a therapy appointment in the afternoon. I've got to be honest. I can't miss that appointment, so that may be a knock-out factor."

"You'll probably have more than one during the week. But it's no problem if they're in the late afternoon. My tech can cover while you're gone, and Sara likes to hang around, too."

She could have hugged him. Kissed him. Not only because he understood the importance of her own schedule but because he offered her a real opportunity in the first place. He treated her as he'd treat anyone else, and if she handled it well, he could be a reference for her in the future. Oh, she definitely wanted this job.

"I'll be there. You said early. How early?"

"You tell me what works for you. There's parking in front of the clinic."

"When does your regular office manager show up?"

"About seven thirty."

"Then I'll be there at seven thirty."

"Great. That's a load off my mind. While Peggy and I are in surgery, we can't worry about the front office."

Hoping she hadn't bitten off more than she could chew, Becca just said, "I'll handle it. And…"

"And what?"

"And thanks. Thanks for thinking of me."

"Funny you should say that. My challenge has become *not* thinking of you."

Seemed like she wasn't the only one distracted with daydreams.

#

Two kitties lounged on the shelves of a wooden "tree" built against the reception room wall while a big ball of yellow fluff strolled along the cat walk above them.

"Butterscotch always wants to lord it over the rest," explained Sara, pointing to the big boy while slipping on her backpack. "Everyone knows him. Hope you like it here. I gotta catch the bus, so see ya later. Bye, Daddy." Her last words rang through the air while the child ran out the clinic door. Ran so fast Becca barely had time to say good-bye.

Adam had greeted her earlier, the door wide open, his eyes shining, and looking so professional—so handsome—in his white coat and stethoscope around his neck. Whether his good spirits were because of her in particular or because he'd gotten coverage for his office at the last minute, she didn't know. She hadn't expected to feel the warmth that radiated through her body when she'd seen him. Her face might even have become apple red. She had to admit that this man shook her up—in a good way.

He'd started explaining the routines at a rapid pace, giving her a tour at the same time, but was interrupted when patients began showing up. Becca retreated behind the reception desk.

"Just show me any forms they need to complete for now. If you'll give me the sign-in and password for the computer, I'll try to figure out how to use the programs."

"And this is why I need office wives," he muttered. "Peggy, can you give Rebecca the information she needs?"

Peggy waved him off. He nodded and disappeared through an adjacent door. "You'll be great," the tech said to Rebecca. "I'll show you the ropes as soon as I can, but it'll probably be in the afternoon. I assist Adam all through surgery. Welcome. I'm glad you could cover."

"Thanks." Within the first hour, she greeted a half-dozen surgical patients and their owners, all of whom wanted to know what had happened to Arlene Farr. Becca considered it an icebreaker as she explained the woman's absence, explained post-op phone calls, and held the leashes or cat carriers until Peggy could take the animals to the back.

So far, so good in this new world of veterinary medicine. New but somehow familiar. As with human medicine, the focus was on the patient. Four legs, two legs…so what? A patient was a patient. She wanted to cuddle them all but remembered what Adam had said about the pet parents and paid attention to the owners before petting their babies. The poor humans were as worried about their pets as any mom or dad would be about their child. Who knew?

"She's got a mass right there," said one owner, placing Becca's fingers on the small bulge. Becca nodded and said, "We'll call as soon as the surgery's over." Then, to cover her bases, added, "There are several surgeries today, so hang tight. You'll get a call as soon as possible."

The man nodded, leaned over to hug his golden lab. "Be a good girl, Jessie." He looked at Becca. "She's my family, ya know."

Becca nodded, her throat tight. "We'll take good care of her." She held her hand for the dog to sniff and then reached for the leash. "C'mon, girl." The golden sniffed a bit longer, then walked alongside Becca as if she'd known her forever.

Becca winked at Jessie's owner and led the dog to the back, hoping to meet up with Peggy right away. But it was Adam who spotted her first. "Great job. Jessie's very particular, aren't you, girl?" He scratched her behind the ears.

"Her owner's worried," said Becca.

"Every pet parent worries. We have a laboratory right on site, so he'll know the status today. I'll give you a grand tour later on."

"I'd like that." As she left him near the treatment area, she realized that this was the first time she'd been on his turf. All their interactions until now had been at Sea View House or in a public sphere. Today, he'd invited her inside his world. It had to have been intentional. They both knew, but hadn't acknowledged, that instead of calling Rebecca, he could have called an employment agency and gotten a registered temp worker.

#

Sweating hard, Becca left the rehab center that afternoon and got into her car. Almost a duplicate of her day in Boston, she'd put in an intense session and was in no shape to return to Adam's place. Maybe he'd have to replace her.

"I've got Sara now as well as Peggy," Adam said when she called. "And, of course, Ginger's here, too. So go home."

"I'll stay later tomorrow," Becca promised, picturing the grey in the reception area.

"You'll make that decision tomorrow. See you in the morning."

"First tell me...what's Ginger's job?"

His deep, mellow laugh sent shivers throughout her body. She squeezed her lids shut and pictured Adam with his head thrown back and eyes gleaming. She could barely breathe.

"That racer's turning into an office pet. Butterscotch has some competition."

She liked that he found humor in the little things, if cats and dogs living together could be called a little thing. But for God's sake, she had to stop turning Adam into something special. He wasn't a knight in shining armor. And she didn't need any rescuing. Adam was just a single parent trying to make a good life for his child.

Her mom had tried to do the same for Becca. But she and Sara would have different memories of their upbringing. Not only in the details but in the atmosphere. Worry versus joy. Money counted. Education counted. And no one would call her mom an optimist. So attitude counted, too. Sara was lucky to have a dad who knew how to laugh.

Becca's duties became routine within a few days. She liked being at work, loved the patients, and was inventive in figuring out ways to reach high or low items. She saw why Adam's practice thrived. His attention to both the patients and their owners revealed the passion for his work. But nothing revealed it more than when he showed her the plans for his new expansion on the Friday evening a week after she'd started working. All the patients were gone. Sara was gone, too, with Katie for a softball practice. Adam would pick them up at the local pizza place afterwards.

As Becca studied the blueprints on his desk and listened to Adam speak about his future plans, she knew he'd move heaven and earth to provide an adoption kennel for his beloved greyhounds right in Pilgrim Cove.

"I'll hear one way or another about my funding very soon, any day now. I'm investing some of my own money, too, but it's not enough for a build-out done right. So I applied to the Retired Greyhound Foundation for the rest."

He deserved the money. Not only was his heart in the project but his mind, too. His blueprints showed his attention to both the big items and the small, with large separate runs for each dog, at the end of which would be a big, soft bed. Easy access to the fenced-in yard behind the clinic, where the dogs could run as much as they liked. Automatic sliding doors to the turnout area where they'd relieve themselves. Trench drains, hoses, rubber mats, everything needed for a clean operation. And a state-of-the-art surveillance system.

"You'll need a larger staff," Becca said as she browsed the plans.

"I'm going to recruit volunteers," Adam replied. "I need to hold operating costs down since construction is the big item. But you're right. I'll have to have someone here overnight."

"Well, it can't be you," Becca said quickly, "or you won't be able to function."

"I agree with half your statement. It won't be me." His eyes narrowed, and a quizzical expression crossed his face. "I could manage, but did you think I'd leave Sara alone in the house at night?"

"No! Of course not," said Becca. "I—I guess I forgot about her. I was just thinking about you."

He didn't respond for a moment, then a frown settled on his forehead. He stepped away from the desk. "Sara and I...you know...we're a package deal."

Becca gasped. "I never meant otherwise. Good God, Adam, I was brought up by a single mom. Do you think I don't know how it feels to want security and reassurance? Sara is a delight. Would I ever separate a parent...."

She didn't continue. Couldn't. Adam's lips covered hers—hard, demanding. His arms came around her, and she leaned in. His mouth softened and trailed up and down her neck. She shivered, moaned, and cupped his cheeks, searching for more. Nothing else mattered but another kiss. His tongue stroked her lips, and she opened them for a more satisfying taste. Their tongues teased, danced, and explored, until he drew back, panting.

She watched his chest rise and fall, knowing hers did the same. "Adam...?

"You're turning my world upside down. So, unless you want to finish this...we need to stop now."

His world? What about hers? Every idea she'd had about her future since the bombing had just been blown away.

"I—I don't want to stop, but I think for now we'll just have to say, 'to be continued.'"

His slow smile spread warmth to every nook and cranny in her body. When he reached for her, she allowed herself to be drawn. She fit right beneath his chin and, with her ear against his chest, heard the strong, steady beat of his heart. Steady, dependable. Just like the man himself.

CHAPTER SIX

As soon as the ferry docked the next morning, Becca got out of her car and waited for Josie and Nick to come ashore. Her cousin was true-blue, had stuck to her word to return on the weekend, bringing Nick this time. Becca approved. Nick was a smart guy with a blossoming career in finance. Most important, he was as crazy about Josie as she was about him, and that was what counted.

"So, you're doing all right?" asked Nick, embracing her as gently as he'd touch a porcelain doll.

"I'm fine, Nick. And strong. Now, give me a real hug, like you mean it." He laughed and pressed her closer. "I'm so glad you're both here." If she wanted relationships to get back on track, Becca knew she had to take the lead. Ordinarily, Nick was in and out of their apartment in Boston, and at this point, Becca considered him almost a brother.

"I'm really happy to see you both," Becca repeated, leading them to the car. "But where are your bags?"

Josie tapped her tote. "We've got odds and ends in here. Unfortunately, we're only staying for the day this time. We'll boat back tonight after we do the grocery shopping and…"

"Not necessary," Becca interrupted. "I can do it on my own." She grinned. "I'm glad I qualified for Sea View House. I like it here."

"Wow!" said Josie, shaking her head. "What a difference two weeks makes."

"From what Josie said," added Nick, "I expected to find you sort of tired…maybe scared or lonely…"

Becca pulled into her driveway and waited for the couple to join her on the pavement. "Just look at the old girl, Nick," she said, waving toward the house. "How could I be scared in a strong vessel like that? My energy's come back, too. It seems the harder I exercise, the more energy I have."

"That's good. It's great! Glad you're happy here." He nodded at Josie. "So, maybe we should tell her now."

Becca froze. No surprises, please. No more changes. She took a breath. "Tell me what?"

"One of those odds and ends in my tote bag," said Josie as they all walked down the driveway to the back porch, "is a bottle of champagne."

Becca didn't need a genius IQ to figure out where Josie was taking the conversation. "Congratulations! Now, tell me more. Tell me everything."

Josie put her bag down on the redwood table and waved her left hand slowly in front of Becca. The ring on her fourth finger twinkled the way a diamond should. "Nick asked, and I said yes. It was very romantic… *He* was very romantic." She looked at her fiancé. "Can I tell her about it?"

He shrugged, grinned, and planted a kiss on Josie's cheek. "Have fun. I'm going inside for a minute. I'll find glasses."

"Can we drink it with lunch?" asked Becca with a laugh. "Bring out the burgers, Nick, and fire up the grill.

Since you're not staying overnight, we'll eat dinner at lunchtime."

She sat on the bench and turned toward her cousin. "That should keep him busy. Now tell me everything."

With the front of her mind, Becca listened to Josie's tale of Nick on bended knee in Boston Garden, of the laughter and tears, of the happiness. In the back of her mind, however, lay the looming question of her own future. She'd be alone now. Totally on her own after her stay in Pilgrim Cove.

"I'm still searching for the right apartment," said Josie when she finished her own happy tale. "I'd never leave you in the lurch." She patted Becca's shoulder and added, "but I'll only be sharing it for about six months. We're planning a spring wedding. A time of new beginnings."

Josie was being kind. So was Nick. Her cousin didn't need a new apartment. She could join Nick at any time. Sticking with Becca for now was Josie's loving way.

"I think we should change the specs to a one bedroom," said Becca. "I can't afford two bedrooms on my own, and I certainly don't want to do another apartment search so soon after this one."

"Just what I hoped you'd say," said Josie. "Smaller might be easier to find. I actually have a couple of leads to follow next week."

She should have been eager, but without Josie to share costs, a shadow stained Becca's optimism. She promptly dismissed her financial worries for the moment. She'd think about them later. Today called for celebration. She grinned at her guests. "You two aren't the only ones with a surprise."

"Go on," said Josie. "I think you're about to burst."

"I've got a job! A temporary job."

If Josie's eyes widened any farther, they'd pop out of her head. "Wow! We've got a lot to celebrate. Spill it, Becca. Spill those Boston beans."

So she did. "But temp jobs are just that. And they don't pay what I earned at the hospital."

Josie waved Becca's words away. "I heard more about Adam Fielding than I did about your responsibilities." Her eyes gleamed. "Adam does this, Adam does that, the patients love him, he's going to enlarge his clinic, and his daughter's so sweet...." She paused and leaned down. "He seemed like a nice guy when I met him, so, what's going on, Bec?"

"Nothing to—"

"I don't like it," interrupted Nick, starting to pace. "He could be taking advantage of you. Invite him for lunch. I'll share my burgers."

Becca felt her face flame. The kisses she and Adam had exchanged had not required any coercion on Adam's part. She'd ridden the wave with him without regret. Still had no regrets. But that part of her life was private. Their relationship was new, fragile, just developing.

"Let's make this a family visit," she said, dismissing Nick's concerns.

#

Becca stood on the dock that evening, waving good-bye to her guests until the boat departed for Rowes Wharf in Boston. The afternoon had passed quickly, the conversation never stopping. They'd walked across the sand together, Becca using her cane, until they'd reached the shoreline where the sand was hard packed. Then she'd folded the cane, and they'd continued to walk. She could have been anyone. She rejoiced in being ordinary.

"The water's tempting," said Nick. "Mind if I take a quick swim?"

"Of course not," said Becca. "Go, go. Enjoy yourself. I want you guys to have fun and come back for another visit."

"No problem about that!" Nick raced into the water.

Josie stared after him. "He's got a point. It's gotten warmer this week, and the summer's just starting. You're always covered up, Bec. Long pants, long skirts. Won't you be cooler wearing shorts?"

"Cotton skirts are cooler than you think. Light material, soft and fluid…the air flows…" Her words trailed away.

Josie squeezed her hand. "Your leg is nothing to be ashamed of, Bec. You see the returning soldiers on television all the time. Men and women. They've got prosthetics, too. Everything's out in the open these days."

Choosing what to wear used to be so simple, but nothing remained simple anymore. "I'm not ashamed, Jo. I did wear shorts—one day early in the week—and people stared. Strangers came right up to me. 'So you're the heroine,' they'd say. They'd ask a lot of questions, wish me luck, and rush off."

She took a deep breath. "I knew exactly what they were thinking. If it could happen to this ordinary girl, it could happen to them. Let's change the subject. I don't want to talk about it; I just want to forget."

"Forget? Are you kidding?" Josie's voice squeaked.

If Becca had said she was from Mars, her cousin would have sounded the same. "Well…maybe I'm exaggerating. Of course, I'll never forget, but I'm tired of all these conversations—they pull me backwards. Whatever happened to 'Hi. Nice weather we're having'?"

Josie burst out laughing. Becca joined in. Maybe she was being ridiculous, but it felt good. It felt right laughing with Josie. She couldn't count the number of times they'd giggled themselves to sleep when they were kids, visiting at each other's homes.

Kids. She quieted down and stared at the ocean. In the near distance, boats cruised parallel to the shore. Pleasure craft. Some folks fishing, some searching for a cove in which to anchor and maybe have a picnic lunch. Some, like Nick, went swimming. All enjoyed being on and in the water.

"And then there are the children," Becca said quietly. "Look at how many kids are on the beach. I don't want to scare them."

Especially not Sara. That little sensitive girl probably couldn't handle it. Not without guidance.

"Kids are resilient," said Josie. "Give them a basic explanation, and they'll accept it. Just like we do with the kids in Pedi."

Her cousin might have made a point, but… "Maybe."

"Not maybe. I'm right. As for the other stuff…people are people. They're curious. But I agree, they shouldn't be getting in your face."

"Thanks. The attack was prime-time television and headline news for weeks. But I just don't want to relive it."

Josie remained quiet, and so did Becca. They waved to Nick as he jumped waves and then returned to shore.

Now, after a wonderful day with her cousin and promises to return lingering in her ears, Becca left the pier and headed home. In retrospect, Nick had amused her, at times acting like the quintessential big brother, curious about this Adam fellow and warning Becca to be careful. At other times, he was so focused on Josie he probably forgot Becca existed. Love. It could make a person giddy.

Becca dismissed Nick's fears about Adam. The thought of the vet taking unfair advantage of her was ridiculous. She possessed nothing that Adam would want, let alone scheme to get. She could offer him computer and administrative skills. And friendship. He'd given her a job, a kangaroo apron, and introduced her to a world of beautiful greyhounds. Beautiful to look at and wonderful companions. Ginger was proof! Nick was off base. Maybe his attitude was a guy thing, too.

Once back at Sea View House, she tackled her laundry. More than a week's worth had piled up, so it really couldn't wait. In her bedroom, she filled the basket halfway and hefted it to her waist. She carried it instead of rolling it on a chair. Two trips to the machine and all her dirty clothes were tumbling in warm, soapy water, just as they should be. Becca stared through the glass door at the kaleidoscope of colors going round and round. Laundry was certainly a boring chore until it became a challenge. A challenge she'd just met. Maybe not worthy of champagne, but the effect was the same. A little bubble of satisfaction infused her. She'd had a great day. She'd managed to do her laundry and walk on the beach!

Reaching for the phone, she searched for Adam's number. Good news was something to share. She listened as it rang once, twice, three times and finally left a message. Hmm…it was Saturday night. What did she expect? Most singles would be out and about, looking for a little fun on a weekend evening. Hadn't she first seen Adam at the Wayside Inn bar on a Friday night? He was probably out with friends again. Sara was probably with Katie. While she—Becca—stayed home, doing laundry. The new normal? Sighing heavily, she bit her lip as a wave of sadness threatened to roll through her.

No pity parties allowed! She'd had a great day. In fact, she'd had a great week. Working at the clinic proved she could hold a job as well as earn a few bucks; going to physical therapy had upped her confidence level. Next time, she might add swimming to her regimen. The local therapists wanted her in the pool, but she'd objected to the idea on the spot. Cautious, as usual, since the bombing. Swimming was a whole 'nother environment. One she needed to control and needed time to figure out.

Her life was full. So what if she was folding clothes on a Saturday night? They were her clothes, and she'd laundered them without help.

And then she heard a knock at the door.

"Are you home?" She recognized Adam's voice immediately. "I want you to meet a couple new friends of mine."

#

Friends? Her kitchen was a mess, not an empty surface to be found. She had no cake in the house. And no more champagne. Oh, well…too bad.

She opened the door and looked up. Tall, Hazel, and Handsome filled the archway. He had a scruffy look, his hair messed up, but a smile wide and inviting. He leaned over and kissed her. Oh. The night was getting better.

"Meet Honey and Duke," said Adam. "They're brother and sister from the same litter."

It was only then that she saw the two unfamiliar greyhounds at Adam's side. Both brindle in color and quiet, they'd blended into the dusky evening. Sara and Ginger stood at Adam's other side.

"Holy Toledo. Three! That's a lot of dog." Becca smiled and stepped toward the child. "Hi, Sara. I see Ginger's still the one for you." She scratched Ginger behind the ears, leaned down for a dog kiss.

"She's my favorite and she's mine. For keeps. Daddy said so."

Becca had no problem believing the girl. Surely in this arena, Adam would deny her nothing.

"And you like Ginger, too, don't you?" asked Sara.

"Of course I do. She's a sweetheart." *Just like you.*

"Sara seems to be collecting a lot of sisters these days," said Adam, "including a really older sister." His pointed glance at Becca was unmistakable.

"Me?" A corner of her heart opened. She knew this child, knew about the emptiness inside when a parent was missing. Becca's daydreams of her own dad had never filled the void. Little Sara had memories of a loving mom, but she also had a void now, too.

Becca turned to the girl, opened her arms, and Sara stepped inside. Her arms closed gently around the child. So little-girl sweet. If acting as a big sister for the summer would make Sara happy, give her more confidence, then Becca was up for it. "I'm very flattered, my little Snow White."

"Huh?"

Becca chuckled. "When I met you and Katie for the very first time, I thought Snow White and Cinderella had waltzed into the room."

"But no wicked stepmothers."

"Just one very pregnant mother."

Sara giggled. Becca laughed. And Adam steered them all outside. "C'mon. This 'whole lot of dog' is too much for your kitchen."

Becca turned her attention back to the greys. Three. The two new ones seemed a bit restless and stuck to Adam's side. Another thought came. Could it be…? She pivoted toward the vet. "Adam! Did you get the money? Does this mean you're expanding now?"

"I'm glad about your excitement, but sorry to say, not yet. Soon. In the meantime, I'll continue to work with one or two at a time in my house. We drove to Boston today to get these two couch potatoes."

"Couch potatoes?" asked Becca. "You've got to be kidding."

But Adam just grinned, and Sara said, as if quoting a book, "Greyhounds are the big dogs that live small."

"The goal is to transition them from racing dogs to family pets," said Adam. "These dogs are smart. They're used to being handled by people and being with other dogs. So the transition is not too hard if the new owner is smart, too. Even though greys have a lot to learn about living in a house, they adjust fairly easily."

All very interesting, but Adam wasn't exactly meeting her eye as he spoke. A new suspicion reared, and if she were correct, she'd stop him now.

"Nice try, Doc, but I'm not adopting a dog. So, just get that right out of your head."

To his credit, he now met her gaze head on. "Rebecca, honey, if that was my goal, I would have said it right out. I would have talked you around. But I've got more respect for you than that. Nope, I've got something else in mind."

Before he could continue, Sara burst out, "Ms. Rebecca, can Ginger spend the night with you and part of tomorrow, too? Daddy and I have to work with Honey and Duke, but Ginger still needs attention."

Becca glanced at Adam. "Coward. Making a child do the dirty work."

"Never said a word to her," he replied with a grin. He tousled Sara's hair. "But good job, sweetheart. You know Ms. Rebecca is a softie inside. I bet she'll say yes."

How could she not when Ginger, as usual, had inserted herself between Sara and Becca, nuzzling one, then the other, happy to be with her human girlfriends?

"Of course she can. And I bet your dad brought her bowls and kibble, too. Must be in that backpack he's wearing."

Sara giggled. "You're right, and I'm so glad. You're the only one I'd let Ginger stay with. And maybe next time, I can sleep over, too."

Next time? "That would be fun." Becca forced a smile, a myriad of issues passing through her mind. The prosthesis. What if Sara needed her in the middle of the night? Becca would be on crutches or in the wheelchair. Lots of questions and explanations. Oh, no. Not a good idea. She'd have to create excuses if Sara asked again.

CHAPTER SEVEN

"Ginger's fine, honey. She slept at the foot of my bed all night. And she already went out and tinkled in the backyard." Rebecca spoke into the phone, yawning at the same time.

"Tinkled?" Sara paused. "Oh, you mean urinated. That's the real word. There's a lot of science around my house. And a lot of vocabulary words."

"I bet there is. Are you up extra early?"

"Nope. Everyone's up. It's already seven o'clock."

Not everyone. Ginger was snoozing again on Becca's bed, and Becca had every intention of joining her.

"Daddy said we're all going out for brunch. To the Diner on the Dunes. I love that place. So be ready at nine o'clock. Wait, wait. He's calling me."

Becca looked at the phone. Either the sweet child had turned into Napoleon leading the troops or her dad was working behind the scenes.

The next voice she heard was Adam's.

"I thought I should take over before she blew it completely."

"I second that suggestion."

"The Diner is really excellent, with an extensive menu. You're sure to find something you like. So, would you like to join us for Sunday brunch?" he asked.

Tempting on several fronts, especially when she detected the eagerness as he spoke. "Is going back to bed for a while an option?"

"Uh-oh. Did you have a bad night? Ginger keep you up?"

"Just the opposite. I had the best night's sleep since I arrived at Sea View House. I guess Ginger and I were both tired. She's still on my bed, snoring. I'm jealous."

"So am I," Adam said, his quiet words soaked with meaning.

In an instant, Becca's fatigue disappeared. She pictured Adam in her bed, their arms intertwined, kisses given and received. Her breath hitched; her grip on the phone tightened. "Interesting idea," she whispered. "Pick me up at nine. I'll be ready."

"I'm more than ready right now."

She disconnected. Wouldn't touch that last remark.

Two hours later, exactly on time, Adam slouched at her back door, looking as male and sexy as any rodeo cowboy. "Good morning, Rebecca," he drawled.

She basked in his growing smile, gleaming eyes, and overall visage of happiness. He must have sensed her reaction. Without hesitating, he leaned toward her, blocking the morning light as his kiss fanned the sparks ignited earlier. Her tongue met his, and he wrapped his arms around her, closing whatever gap existed between them.

He was strong but gentle. She shifted, stretched, and moved into him, totally absorbing his touch. Never worried about keeping her balance. Never thought at all! Feelings overrode reason, and lightness filled her. Of spirit, body, and mind. She floated like a feather in the wind. This man. This tall, hazel, and handsome guy....

She trusted him.

As the realization hit, she pulled away and stared at Adam as though she'd never seen him before. Trust was not a small thing. It was everything. And she couldn't explain how or why or when her trust in him had sprouted and grown. Why him? Why now? She'd had an active social life in Boston, but no one had captured her serious attention before Adam. No one had made her heart pound like Adam. No one had excited her like Adam.

"What?" he asked. "What's wrong? Do I have dog hair on my shirt?"

She shook her head. "I-I don't usually wake up to a 'good morning' like that."

"Neither do I." His tone held wonder, and his eyes shone with a hopeful glint.

Seemed they were both at the starting gate together.

"I'm ready," said Becca. "Ready to begin a new day." Perhaps a new life.

#

The Diner on the Dunes was a one-story white clapboard affair, with a row of porthole-like windows near the roofline. Becca fully expected a nautical theme to follow inside.

"We might run into a few of the ROMEOs," said Adam, pulling into the crowded parking lot. "Notice the sign in the doorway when we get there."

"I hope Katie's here with Papa Bart," Sara added from the backseat of the SUV.

"It's possible," said Adam, shutting off the ignition. He turned toward Becca. "Wait for me. This vehicle is higher than a regular car. Don't get down on your own.

Not yet." He turned to his daughter. "And you stand right at the side of the car. No running ahead."

"I know." She sighed dramatically. "I'm not a baby."

Becca opened her passenger door and wondered how she'd agreed not to drive. Why she'd agreed to this arrangement. Must've been too many kisses. She swallowed her laughter, but Adam had already walked around the vehicle and caught her tiny smile.

"What?"

"Not important." She swiveled sideways on the seat a little at a time so that she faced outward. Scooting her bottom to the edge until both feet touched the pavement, she put her hand in Adam's. "Let's do it."

Strong and steady, he provided just the right amount of support so that she stood firmly on her feet. "All right! Good job, Becca," she cheered.

"Excellent job," said Adam. "But do you often talk to yourself?"

She had to think. "I guess I do. Since the"—she glanced toward Sara—"bombing," she whispered. "I guess talking out loud keeps me focused. Do I sound crazy?"

"I vote for whatever works. And by the way, Sara knows about the marathon. We were watching it on and off that day on television."

But how much did she know? Was she aware of Becca's involvement? Now was not the time or place for that discussion.

As they approached the entrance to the diner, Becca pointed and laughed. "I see what you mean." Above the doorway was a bold red-and-white wooden sign that read *Home of the ROMEOs.*

"Nothing shy about our boys," sighed Adam. "And they don't go hungry! Between the Diner and the Lobster Pot, they've got the whole day covered."

"Lucky they don't weigh five hundred pounds."

"Never happen. They walk. They patrol. They cover a few miles almost every day. And Bart still works his real estate. The others take on contract jobs."

"Contract jobs?" asked Becca. "Wait a minute, just a minute. Maybe they'd volunteer some time with your new expansion. When you get more dogs."

He rewarded her with a quick kiss, observed by a little girl with big brown eyes. Another topic for later discussion. Having a child was a bigger responsibility than Becca had realized. A twenty-four/seven responsibility. Whatever she and Adam said or did had the power to affect Sara. *Well, sweetheart, life hurts. Deal with it.*

Ouch! She winced as her mom's philosophy popped into her head and reminded herself that she was not her mother. Becca was more attuned to kids and would never cause Sara any emotional pain. Would never make the same financial mistakes Angela had made. She shivered as shadow images of her mother's hasty second marriage flowed through her memory bank.

As they approached the diner, the aroma of coffee made Becca's stomach growl. "I hope we get a table right away."

The place was big and bright. Booths lined two walls, and a counter ran along the third. Tables and chairs filled the center of the floor, each one occupied with hungry diners.

"Too bad. It looks like we'll have to wait," said Becca.

As she spoke, from the far end of the restaurant came the unmistakable and eager voice of Bart Quinn. "Ahoy, Sea View House. There's room for ya here!"

And there was Katie rushing toward Sara. "C'mon, Sara. You'll sit with me."

"Outmaneuvered," joked Becca, seeing Adam's face light up as he watched the girls.

"Do you mind joining the crowd?"

"Of course not. That old curmudgeon may turn out to be my best friend yet."

"Best friend? Now you're hurting my feelings."

She loved the easy give-and-take between them, his easy manner with her and how he took everything in stride. Like he was handpicked for her.

They arrived at the large, round corner booth— almost filled with ROMEOs and wives. Chief O'Brien and Dee, Doc Rosen and Marsha, Lou Goodman, the librarian, and his wife, Pearl. And Sam Parker, Katie's other grandfather. In the middle of the table stood a *Reserved* sign. "Reserved for the ROMEOs."

"You've got clout," said Rebecca as she sat on the chair Adam held for her.

"Only for breakfast," said Dee. "I used to manage this place. I hid the sign as soon as they left their table. More often than not, I had to shoo them out the door."

"But not too quickly," said Chief O'Brien, giving his wife a peck on the cheek. "She didn't rush us."

"Wouldn't have mattered if I did," said Dee. "This guy, here, came back five times a day." She imitated a man's low pitch. "Just patrolling the area, Dee. Just checking up. How about a cup of coffee?"

In a flash, Sara stood. "You know what? Daddy and I patrol, too. Sea View House. Every night. And in the daytime, Ms. Rebecca works with us. We've got to check up on her."

Heat seared Becca's face. *Where's a magic wand so I can disappear?*

"And now Ginger lives with her, and you know what else?" Sweet little Sara was sure on a roll.

"I think that's enough..." Becca began.

"What else, lassie?" Bart cut in as smoothly as a warm knife through butter.

"I saw Daddy and Ms. Rebecca kissing this morning. It was cool."

"Sara! Quiet." Adam responded the way Becca wanted to.

"Well, you did," Sara insisted. Seemed Adam's daughter had developed some stubborn in her.

Becca wanted to slide under the table. Instead, she snuck a peek around it. Grins, chuckles, and nods from one retired old man to another. So she did what any woman would do—studied the menu as if her life depended on it. Maybe it did.

#

He hadn't gotten the funding for the new rescue center.

On the following Thursday evening, Adam stared at his computer screen in disbelief. He was in his home office. Sara was in bed, the house quiet for the night. Checking emails was often his last item of business for the day. An ordinary routine. Tonight wasn't ordinary.

Disappointment filled him. Deep, dark disappointment unlike anything he'd recently experienced. The low scores in certain areas of his Request for Proposal had told their own story. In essence, the Foundation praised him, loved his work, but his demographics were poor. His location was too far afield. Pilgrim Cove was out of the way with a small population and little potential for foster homes. His competitors for the funding drew from bigger areas that offered a greater chance of attracting adoptees. They offered a greater probability of other veterinarian volunteer partnerships, as well.

Damn it! He thought of all the blueprints he'd had drawn up by an architect experienced with veterinary clinics. He'd laid out his own money for that. He thought about all the hours he'd put into this dream. All the planning. All the sharing. And Sara! She'd looked forward to this new adventure, too. Damn it again.

Another email pinged in. This one looked personal. Direct from the head of the awards committee at the Greyhound Foundation. Adam had met the fellow a time or two in the past.

"Want to soften the blow?" Adam murmured as he began scanning the post. When he was finished, he sat back in his leather chair and rested his head against its tall back. The irony did not escape him. A job. They were offering him a job. Full-time in the Boston branch of the foundation. They needed him and wanted him. Had he seen the latest headline in the Florida papers?

Raced to Death. Individual stories of individual dogs. It could make a grown man cry. Twenty-one racetracks still operated in the country, thirteen of them in Florida. It had been only a couple of years ago that his own state banned dog racing. Rescue centers were still needed, no doubt about that. And Boston had a large operation. A good operation.

He knew the facts. He loved the dogs. He didn't agree with the results of his application. Dog lovers would come here if he could expand and publicize. The greys would turn Pilgrim Cove into an adoption destination. Would he close his clinic and practice in Boston? Not a chance.

Sara was happy in Pilgrim Cove. They'd moved here because they'd both needed a new beginning after Eileen died. Nope. He'd have to swallow his disappointment. He didn't have the money to go it alone. But he wouldn't uproot his family. Sighing heavily, he supposed a person couldn't have everything.

And now he'd have to tell Sara…and Rebecca. That wonderful, brave, beautiful woman. After all his talk about the expansion…she'd think he was a failure. Or she'd feel sorry for him. Damn it again.

#

The next morning, Becca jingled her keys, and Ginger tracked her every move. Not only had she become the office pet, she'd become Becca's shadow. The dog had remained at Sea View House all week and seemed content to stay put at Becca's side. Adam had brought over a raised feeding platform for the two bowls of food and water and set up a turnout area in the backyard. He cleaned it up, too.

"I guess we're housemates, you beautiful girl, aren't we?" Becca patted the hound. "And I like having you here." She jingled her keys again. "Ready to go to work?"

Ginger marched to her side. Earlier in the week, the hound had seemed forlorn at being left behind. Becca had brought her to the office as an experiment the following day. Butterscotch's reaction was to march back and forth in front of her old friend, tail held high, as if to say, "You can stay, but remember, I'm the boss." Ginger didn't seem to care at all. The dog lay next to Becca's desk most of the time.

Today's routine was no different except that Sara was at the clinic waiting in the reception area with Peggy. "School ended yesterday and camp doesn't start till Monday, so I'm here. Daddy's in his office." She sang, smiled, and danced around the room, hugging Ginger and Becca from time to time.

"Happy girl! Was school so bad?" asked Becca.

"Nope. But summer's better." She cocked her head. "When's Ms. Arlene coming back?"

"I'm not sure. Your dad hasn't said anything."

Peggy chimed in. "At least another week. With a broken hip, her mom still needs help. She might come to Pilgrim Cove to stay with Arlene for a while." She turned to Becca. "Are you okay staying on for another week or so? You're doing a really good job for us."

"Definitely. I'm sorry about her mom, but I'll also be sorry to leave when Arlene returns."

"We're glad you're flexible. Now I've gotta get Lucky ready for his big day, don't I, pooch?" She held a Jack Terrier in her arms. "Let's get some blood work on you," she crooned to him. "See you guys later."

Becca turned to Sara. "So are you my assistant or am I yours?"

The child giggled. "You're so funny. I can't work yet. I'm too young."

Older than your years, sweetie. "You know an awful lot about how a veterinary hospital works."

"I have to. One day Dad and I will have a sign that says *Pilgrim Cove Animal Hospital, Adam Fielding and Daughter*."

The girl was amazing. Becca couldn't remember ever having big dreams like that. "I hope all your dreams come true, Sara. Every single one of them."

Sara nodded and turned away. "That one will," she said, "because Daddy says I can do anything I set my mind to." She glanced shyly at Rebecca and said, "But I have another dream. It's even bigger than that one." She peered over Becca's shoulder, avoiding her glance. "But I can't do that one by myself," she whispered.

Warning bells started to ring in Becca's head. "You're a smart, strong girl, Sara. If you're disappointed, I know you'll be able to deal with it." Once more, shades of Angela Hart made Rebecca wince.

"But I don't want to be disappointed," Sara cried. She ran to Becca and hugged her. "I'm so happy you're here. Daddy's so happy, too. I want you to stay in Pilgrim Cove forever."

She held the girl close while her heart broke for her. Becca couldn't make promises she couldn't keep. "No matter what, Sara, we'll be friends forever, right? Sisters of the heart. You made me that perfect treasure box, and I'll make you one, too." She leaned closer. "Maybe it'll turn out nicer than Katie's."

Sara's nose wrinkled. "That won't be too hard, but I hope you don't have to make it. I hope you stay."

Maybe she'd have to talk to Adam about cooling things down. But when she saw him later that day, he seemed unhappy enough. A bit grumpy, too, which he blamed on a lack of sleep. All thoughts of presenting a possible problem swept from her mind.

#

Becca inserted her gold hoop earrings and stepped back to self-critique. Adam had asked her out for dinner and she'd accepted. He'd regained his usual cheerful demeanor by the next day, and she'd shrugged off his earlier mood. They'd been working together for two weeks now, he'd been to her home several times, and she'd seen him in many guises—dad, boss, vet, community member—but tonight was their first real date. No kids, no dogs. Just them. Papa Bart's Friday night card party with the little girls was coming in handy.

She stared at the big girl in the mirror, the girl with the glowing eyes, whose dark hair cascaded in waves to her shoulders. She approved of the peasant blouse, a colorful print on white. Mostly she approved of the soft weave pants that flowed fluidly when she walked. Fashionable. Comfortable. She wore closed flat shoes. They were cute, but a two-inch sandal would have been better. One day she'd wear heels again. Anything was possible with the new prosthetic building techniques she'd read about. Expensive, but insurance would cover some.

If she'd had any doubts about her appearance, however, they disappeared when she opened the door for Adam. He stood on the threshold and simply stared. His soft whistle expressed more admiration than words. But he managed some of those, too. "You look…you are…so beautiful."

Her eyes misted, and she blinked. Maybe she was hungry, too hungry, for compliments. Maybe she wanted folks to realize she was a regular, ordinary woman. As she gazed into Adam's smiling face, he reached out and stroked her cheek, a sweet and gentle touch. Her heart filled to the brim, and she had her answer.

To him, she was a woman—a normal, everyday woman—whom he seemed to like a lot. His compliments and opinions mattered to her. She loved that he shared them. Adam Fielding mattered more to her than any other man she'd ever been with. He made her laugh, he made her stand taller, and he shouldered responsibility with a pound of common sense. Tall, Hazel, and Handsome had it all, all the qualities she admired. In fact, she couldn't think of anything she disliked about him. Her heart began to race as she faced a new truth.

She was falling in love with Adam.

The realization left her gasping. When he kissed her lightly on the mouth, she couldn't breathe. When he held her hand, her arm tingled. And when a delicious meal was placed before her at the Wayside Inn awhile later, she had no appetite. She was in deep trouble. Focus! She tried to focus on the conversation.

"I'll never give up working with the greys," Adam said, cutting into his steak.

"Of course not." Rebecca reached across the table and squeezed his hands. "I'm so sorry about the funding, Adam. And I'm glad you told me. I couldn't understand why you seemed so sad yesterday. Or maybe out of sorts is the better word. But I-I didn't like it. I was worried."

He slipped her hands inside his larger ones. "You were worried?"

"Well...the atmosphere was different at the clinic today. You were not your usual get-up-and-go self. So I was concerned."

He leaned across the table. "That's a lovely thing for you to say. But I'm sorry I worried you."

"So what will you do now?"

"Turn down their position in Boston. That's for sure. Sara doesn't need any more changes."

Becca felt her smile falter. Boston, with its huge medical complexes, was her home. Her next job would be there. "Sara's a terrific girl, Adam. You're doing a wonderful job."

He shrugged. "We'll find out in about ten years, I guess. With kids, nothing is for sure."

Before she could reply, Becca saw a familiar couple approach. "I think your friends are coming over."

Adam glanced up and stood. He shook hands with the guy. "Rachel and Jack Levine, meet Rebecca Hart, current tenant of Sea View House."

Rachel laughed. "We know who you are, Ms. Hart. We saw you here the first night you arrived. But we're glad to meet you officially now. Actually, very good timing."

Jack took over. "Have you noticed my wife sounds happy? School's out for the year, and she's on vacation...until she starts worrying about next year." He glanced at his watch. "I give her about two hours."

The Levines were a great couple, but more important, very warm to Adam. Another facet of Adam she'd not seen up close before. Friendships.

"Please call me Becca."

"Thanks." Rachel exuded energy and charm. "Do me a favor, and don't listen to Jack. I love my job—I'm assistant principal at the high school—but we're celebrating summer now. The weather's gorgeous, and tomorrow's supposed to be warm and sunny. We're taking the boat out—not for science, just for fun. Swimming, eating. Want to join us?" She looked from Adam to Rebecca. The invitation definitely included both.

A boat? Swimming? Was it safe? Did the woman know about Becca's leg? If she swam, she'd have to remove her prosthesis. In front of strangers. Her stomach tightened. But maybe this was an opportunity…. What to do, what to say. Sweat dotted every pore. The ocean was unpredictable, not as safe as a rehab center pool surrounded by staff. Which she hadn't even gone into yet!

"Rebecca?" Adam's soothing voice. "Come on back."

She focused on his eyes, his warm green eyes. "I don't know, I don't know," she whispered. "What about the waves, the undertow? The Atlantic's mighty powerful…"

Rachel pulled up a chair. "We usually drop anchor in the bay, in a quiet cove we love. We bring a picnic lunch and just relax. Swim when we want to or not at all. Eat when we feel hungry." She threw a loving but mischievous glance at her husband. "Jack's a marine biologist, so the boat's outfitted with all kinds of equipment and supplies. Lots of research goes on there. All types of research…" She grinned and rolled her eyes.

The woman wasn't very subtle, and Becca couldn't help but smile, too.

"See why I called my beauty *Sweet Rachel*?" asked Jack, leaning down and placing a kiss on his wife's neck.

Adam still held Becca's hand, his thumb moving slowly back and forth over hers. "Have I forgotten to add that we're all excellent swimmers, especially Rachel? She trained for the Olympics awhile ago."

Becca stared at her. Tall, slender, with a sleek cap of dark hair. "Is that right?"

"Swimming earned me college scholarships, but in the end, I didn't qualify for the big games."

Broken dreams lay everywhere. Whether in sports or human relationships, high hopes could scatter in a heartbeat. She'd better learn the art of picking up the pieces like Rachel had done. The woman was, as her husband had said, happy.

"So, it's settled then?" asked Jack. "We'll meet at the marina at eleven and stay out a few hours. We'll make sure Sara has fun, too."

"Sara's with Katie overnight," said Adam. "I don't need to be back until three."

The conversation paused while the butterflies in Becca's stomach settled down. "That clinches it," she said with a quick nod. "I'll go. It'll be a practice run…umm, I mean swim."

She'd be a fool to turn down this opportunity. Sara's absence made it perfect. Regardless of her maturity, Sara was still a little girl. Who knew how she'd react when Becca finally got into the water? That is…if she actually did go in.

If? She was an idiot! So what if she was scared? So what if it wasn't a therapy swimming pool? She'd been feasting on the sight and sound of the ocean every night from the backyard at Sea View House, wondering if she'd ever immerse herself in the cool, salty water again.

Now, she had her opportunity. *Grab the brass ring, lassie. Enjoy the ride.* Or the swim.

CHAPTER EIGHT

The docking area of the marina looked like a floating parking lot for boats. Which it was. All sizes and shapes of craft. All purposes, too, from fishing outfits with elevated captain and mate chairs to sailboats and motorboats outfitted strictly for pleasure. They all bobbed merrily in their moorings, reminding Rebecca, as she and Adam walked down the long pier, that her first challenge would be to climb aboard a rocking boat.

She stuck out her chin. "Climbing aboard won't be graceful."

"Who cares?" said Adam. "As long as you get on deck—and I guarantee you will. Write about it in your diary. Make it an adventure."

She peered up at him. "I don't have a diary, but I won't forget about this adventure no matter how it turns out."

Over her bathing suit, Becca wore a white tee shirt and, for the second time in Pilgrim Cove, a pair of denim shorts. Her prosthetic leg was fully visible. In her backpack were two more pair of shorts, a comb, sunscreen, and the special lotions for her skin. Adam carried the bulk of their items—lunch, towels, hats—in his larger pack.

It took her less than five minutes to realize that no one cared about her leg. Everyone was busy with their own preparations for a day on the water.

"I'm an idiot," she said. "All this time, I was afraid to be natural, and look! No one gives a hoot. Maybe if I were a real soldier just back from Afghanistan, I wouldn't give a hoot, either."

Adam came to a dead stop. "You've got to be kidding me. You are exactly like a real soldier except without the fatigues."

Becca had never thought of it that way, despite newspaper coverage of the marathon that focused on the terrorists. She viewed it as an accident caused by two madmen. She'd simply stood in the wrong place at the wrong time.

"And as for these guys," continued Adam, nodding at the crowd on the pier, "everyone's self-absorbed. It's human nature. But don't beat yourself up about being self-conscious. It's only been…what? Two months? That's not a long time to adjust to a trauma." He paused. "God knows it's taken me years to accept Eileen's death. One, two, three, and it was all over. A matter of months."

"I'm so sorry about that." They began walking down the pier again, but this time, clouds darkened her day. "You know what?"

Once more, he halted and gave her his full attention. "What?"

"Life sucks."

"Sometimes." A curt nod underscored his agreement.

Becca swung her arm in a wide arc to encompass the colorful flotilla, the bay, as well as the open water of the Atlantic. "And then…there's this. Not exactly awful, is it?" She beamed up at him.

His stillness raised goose bumps on her arms. An answering smile slowly crossed his face as he studied her. "You've made a point. The scenery is beautiful and gets more beautiful every time I look."

#

"Welcome aboard." Jack Levine extended his hand to Becca while Adam stood closely behind her. It was Becca, however, who figured out how to maneuver. With a minimum of help, she climbed onto the deck—and felt the craft rock. She immediately grabbed Adam's arm.

"A balancing challenge," she said with a laugh. "Good thing I'll be sitting most of the time." Suiting actions to words, she lowered herself to a cushioned bench seat and looked around. "Wow! This isn't just a little dinghy. It's a real ship, and she's gorgeous."

"Actually, this baby is a sports cruiser—thirty feet long with a nine-foot beam," said Rachel, patting a rail. "And built for comfort. Plenty of seating. We can all stretch out if we want to." She looked just as proud of the craft as her husband did.

"If I recall correctly," said Adam, "before he quartered at Sea View House, the captain here used to live on board this floating lab when he trolled for water and mud samples. And fish, too. What a life. Putt-putting around the water up and down the coastline."

"From Nova Scotia to Florida," added Rachel, "quite a coastline. There was a terrible storm while we lived at your house, Becca. I'll never forget that day. It seemed to last forever. And yet, he still goes out for long stretches at a time."

"Fewer and fewer of those trips." Jack untied the ropes that kept *Sweet Rachel* moored to the dock. "I'd rather be home. No more wandering."

A meaningful silence followed that confession. There was a story hiding here. Interesting that Jack and Rachel had both lived at Sea View House. At the same time? Becca wondered about that journal Quinn had mentioned at the beginning of her stay. Maybe she'd take a look.

Five minutes later, they were on the open water, riding parallel to the beach, Jack at the controls. "We've got fishing gear if that interests you."

But Becca barely heard him. The rushing air blew against her face, through her hair. She raised her arms overhead, the sense of speed exhilarating. Her worries vanished. "This feels wonderful. I could ride the wind forever."

"And I could watch you forever," mumbled Adam. He glanced over at his pal. "I think she's enjoying herself."

"I certainly am. So thank you both. Thanks very much for including me."

"Give Adam the credit," said Jack. "It was all his idea."

"A great idea!" Rachel rushed in, glaring at her husband. "We were taking the boat out anyway, and having friends with us makes it more special. So thank you for coming."

The woman couldn't have been more gracious, but Becca stared hard at Adam. "Later, buddy. We'll have this out later." She wasn't a child, and he wasn't responsible for entertaining her. Asking favors of strangers wasn't her way.

But Rachel and Jack Levine weren't strangers to Adam, she realized awhile later, as he took over the controls from his friend and nosed the boat into a quiet cove. Adam seemed as competent and comfortable behind the wheel as his pal, yet didn't seem to own a boat.

"You must have had lessons somewhere," Becca said. "You're very relaxed in the driver's seat."

Adam shrugged. "I grew up near the coast of New Hampshire and fished a lot. Every family had a craft of some kind, including my folks."

"But you don't have one now, do you?"

He chuckled. "I'm not Midas. I can stretch a dollar only so far. Between repaying school loans, running a business, a mortgage on the house, and raising a daughter…" A shadow crossed his face. "I had some extra tucked away for enlarging the clinic had I gotten the foundation's money to help, but"—he shrugged—"that's not happening now."

"A damn shame, too," said Rachel. "You're the best person in the world to care for those greyhounds." She faced Becca and added, "Jack and I are adopting the two he's got now. Honey and Duke. They're so calm and wonderful. And they'll be company for each other when we're at work."

"That's terrific," replied Becca. "The greys are so easy to love. Ginger owns my heart already, and I think she loves me, too. She never leaves my side at home."

"You could have brought her today."

Adam stilled the motor and turned toward them. "Today is for people. No kids, no dogs. Just…us." His warm gaze at Becca made her blush. His definition of "us" was clear to all.

The cove was quiet and almost private. The closest boat was too far away to hail. Becca nodded as she took it all in. No beach or sand here. Trees grew between shelves of rock all along the water's edge.

"Amazing how they thrive in such inhospitable places."

"A bit of rich soil is all the encouragement they need," said Adam. "A little sweetening can go a long way."

The rise of his brow told her he wasn't talking only about trees. But he sat back in his seat, arms at his sides, as relaxed as she'd ever seen him. They had arrived at their cove, but he wasn't going to push her.

"Swim or lunch?" he asked casually.

She'd be a fool to procrastinate. "Swim. Definitely swim," said Becca. "I want to be weightless."

"How can I help you?"

Actually help? No. She had to figure it out herself. "Just stick around and don't laugh at my antics." She glanced over his shoulder. "It's…it's my first time in the water."

"You got it." He shifted his attention to his friends. "Becca and I are going for a swim."

"Then I'm going, too," said Rachel. "I'll get the kickboard and noodles, and Jack will stay on deck and watch us have fun."

In other words, Jack would act as lifeguard. Becca had to ignore the others and concentrate on her tasks at hand. Sitting on the bench, she removed the prosthesis and hoisted herself from the cushions to the deck above her, not too difficult.

"You do that like a pro," said Adam.

She hadn't noticed him watching. His glance traveled between her and the mechanical leg, which she'd placed next to her backpack on the bench, ready to don after her swim.

"I've become a pro." Had he seen her residual limb at all? The stump? Had he seen the scars? Their relationship was moving forward, at some point would become intimate. Then what? Oh, God, what if he pitied her? Her stomach roiled at the thought. Even worse…what if he showed disgust when he finally saw her naked?

Suddenly defensive, she raised her eyes and stuck out her chin. "It is what it is, and I am who I am." She doffed her tee shirt and flung it at him. No point wearing it in the water.

"I love who you are," he replied, catching her shirt with one hand. The words came softly, privately. As though they were alone in Eden, with no one else save God.

But the L word? Had he realized what he'd said? It was too soon. Well…not too soon for her. But how could he know? She…she wasn't the real Becca anymore. She couldn't dance and run and do what she used to, like other women could. She could accept that now, but a guy like Adam, who had everything going for him? Her thoughts swirled, and she looked forward to slipping into the water.

She looked down. Her denim shorts? Yes. She'd keep them on. A comfort level not only for her but maybe for the other three as well. She spun around on her bottom to face the bay and scooted toward the boat's back platform.

"Hang on," called Adam. He walked to her, holding a life vest in his hand. "Want this?"

She'd been a strong swimmer—in the past. Heck, she'd been a good all-around athlete in the past. Now she judged the water's surface. "The bay is calm today. So my answer is…maybe later, if I get tired." A definite maybe.

Adam tossed the vest to Jack. "She'd rather swim than bobble."

Would she ever. She held her breath and pushed off the end of the platform.

She used every muscle and limb she had, including her residual leg. She adjusted her stroke, and it worked.

Then she grasped a kickboard that Rachel had thrown and simply drifted. The weightless feeling was glorious, so glorious she almost ignored her constant shadow. Almost. But she had to admit that having Adam beside her, a big grin on his face, was glorious, too.

"I'm having such fun!" Becca said.

"Hold on to the noodle instead," Adam said, thrusting the floatation device at her. He used one himself and swam closer. She could see the bright green of his eyes—his happy shade. Then the darker one as his intention became clear. One kiss. Then another. And she responded easily, naturally. "So glad you're here. So proud of you," he whispered.

Tears threatened, yet her heart sang. She clung to the noodle and clung to Adam's arm as well. "Thank you. I think I'm proud of me, too." But without Adam, this special day wouldn't have happened. She'd never have felt like an ordinary woman, having a fun time with friends. A lovely day in the water, just like everyone else enjoyed. He'd gone out of his way to provide this for her.

"Come closer," she said. This time she wrapped both her arms around his neck and kissed him with a hunger new to her, a hunger that surprised her. She'd passed the falling-in-love stage. This was the real thing. She loved him, totally loved him. It was so clear now. He was the core of her recent happiness.

She leaned back and stared at the man she'd just trusted with her life. He stared back, eyes glowing, the corner of his mouth heading north. A full smile appeared as he waited. Her heart did a slow tumble…and she knew for sure. "Oh, Adam…"

"Oh, Rebecca…" he mimicked before he kissed her again.

CHAPTER NINE

How could he have gotten this lucky a second time? His relationship with Rebecca was a Technicolor adventure, not a drab, "good enough" kind of connection. No settling for half a loaf, which was what he'd almost done last year with Katie's mom.

Rebecca was special. And Sara was crazy about her. At least, he thought so. Adam listened to the rattle of pans coming from the kitchen as he lay in bed on Father's Day morning. Somehow, Sara had gotten the idea that breakfast in bed was the appropriate gift. He allowed himself a big grin. At most, he and his daughter were good-enough basic cooks who thoroughly appreciated meals at the Diner on the Dunes or the Lobster Pot when they treated themselves. Hmm…maybe he'd reserve a table for that evening, a table for three. Father's Day would be busy, but if he called early enough… He reached for the phone. Rebecca would be up by now.

"Happy Father's Day to you," Sara crooned as she entered his room, a full tray in hand and Honey and Duke on either side of her. He replaced the receiver in its cradle. The child was a magnet for every dog they brought home. With her high grades and her natural abilities…veterinary school could become a reality later on. If her grades and dreams remained constant.

"Thank you, sweetheart." Adam looked at the tray. There was enough French toast for four people. But his eye went directly to the oversized card, definitely homemade, unique, and a kiss to the heart. On the outside, she'd printed *Happy Father's Day* with a photo of Sara and him, with Butterscotch riding on his shoulders. On the inside, she'd written, *I Love You, from Sara and all the kids.*

She'd drawn a picture of every grey they'd taken in from the beginning of the year, printed each name and who'd adopted them. Her art was fantastic. Whether they were parti-colored, solid, or brindle, she'd perfectly captured each one of their temporary visitors.

"Wow," he said. "Just wow."

"You like it?"

"I love it. But I love you more!"

That slow smile. When he saw Sara's smile, when he saw the love for him in her eyes, he could have lassoed the moon for her had she wanted it. His daughter was amazing. And she loved greyhounds as much as he did. Once more, he winced at not getting the funding to expand.

He glanced at the tray again. "Two forks. Smart girl."

She giggled. "Two plates, too. Look underneath." She cocked her head and added. "It could have been three plates, but Ms. Rebecca said you weren't her dad. She's so funny."

"Oh? You invited Rebecca to breakfast?" This sounded promising.

"Yup. She makes you happy."

115

Suddenly, he was on shakier ground. They both were. He finished a bite of toast. "I am happy, Sara. I'm happy with you." It wasn't a child's job to make a parent happy.

"I know, I know. But…but Ms. Rebecca makes you happi*er*!" Her voice rose with emphasis on the final syllable, and hope shone on her face. "I know she does. We always visit her and you wear cologne when we go."

Outed by aftershave. He couldn't deny those items, but he shook his head. It was too soon to know the future. Despite their growing relationship, Rebecca had a big to-do list ahead of her. He wasn't sure exactly where he fit in. Or, in the end, if he'd fit in. Shadows of the past haunted him. Rational or not, sometimes he felt snake bitten. He'd lost Eileen; he'd lost Lila Parker when Jason had come home. Rebecca was wonderful. His feelings were growing every day. But was the third time the charm or the third strikeout?

The day stretched before them. A leisurely Sunday. "She missed breakfast, so how about I invite Rebecca for dinner with us?" He sat at the side of the bed, ready to get up.

"Here?" Sara scanned the room, then went to the door, searching. She turned back to Adam. "She might trip. We've got too many dog toys and other stuff all over."

His daughter had a point. "Then I guess our work is cut out for us." He could make a reservation at the Lobster Pot, but the idea of Rebecca spending time in his home for a change appealed to him. She'd been to his clinic, of course, but today would be the first visit at the house. Fortunately, he knew how to grill a steak.

Adam's house sat next door to the clinic by twenty yards, but Becca had not paid much attention to it before. Now she got out of her car and, with Ginger leashed and at her side, started up the walkway carrying

116

a small gift as well as her contribution to the meal. She glanced ahead and immediately fell in love with the front porch. Since moving to Sea View House, she'd become a sucker for porches. Whether front or back, beach view or town view, a porch welcomed a person home. Especially when a little girl sat on the steps, waiting.

Sara jumped up, waved, and pivoted toward the screen door. "Da-a-d," she called in a sing-song voice, "Ms. Rebecca's here! And she's got a balloon for you." She disappeared inside.

Sara's excitement matched the affection in Becca's heart. Lovely child, and so easy to love. No wonder Bart's family embraced her as Katie's friend.

Becca studied the house for a moment. A traditional Cape Cod with white siding and blue shutters, lanterns hanging on each side of the door. The porch ran almost the entire length of the house with white pillars spaced intermittently. Several cushioned chairs and a low table made the space inviting. Smart to have both the house and clinic fit into the décor of the neighborhood.

The door opened, and a conflagration of humans and canines were meeting and greeting each other. Sara hugged Ginger like a long-lost sister, while Honey and Duke investigated Becca. But no one outshone Adam in Becca's eyes. In a green jersey, hair damp from a shower, and a grin on his face, he gathered her to him for a quick kiss.

"Welcome. Welcome to the madhouse."

"Happy Father's Day," she said, handing him the large, colorful helium-filled balloon. "And it's not a madhouse, it's a wonderful house…maybe a bit busy, but wonderful."

His quiet laughter warmed her. "Kids, dogs…hard to keep up. And I've been told the place could use a decorator, but…Sara and I are comfortable."

"And the greyhounds?"

"They don't get a vote."

Neither the dogs nor the humans could complain. The house was spacious with three bedrooms—one Adam's home office—a large living room, and a kitchen-dining combination with a table that could accommodate eight people. The kitchen door led to another porch at the back of the house and a fenced-in yard. Perfect for a family, but certainly not large enough for a rescue center. Neither was his current clinic.

Becca handed him a package. "A little something with the meal. One item needs refrigeration, and the other needs the freezer."

Adam looked inside the brown grocery bag. "A perfect combo. Ice cream and a six-pack of Sam Adams. What a woman!"

She felt herself blush but enjoyed the gentle teasing.

"I made snacks," said Sara. "Dad says chips and dip aren't called hors d'oeuvres, but we also have cheese and crackers. Katie's mom calls that an hors d'oeuvres."

Pretending to be the woman of the house. Trying the role on for size. And doing a darn good job. "Sounds right to me," said Becca.

"Can we have our hors d'oeuvres on the back porch and leave the dogs inside?" Sara looked anxiously from Becca to her dad.

"A wonderful idea," said Becca. "I love porches!"

Adam decided he loved seeing Becca on his porch. On the double swing with Sara while he grilled their steaks. He hadn't had a special female guest in his home for a long time. He'd preferred the single dad family lifestyle, but Becca was special. She was a siren song, constantly on his mind.

He tuned into the female conversation.

"Ms. Rebecca, can I ask you something?"

"Sure, Sara. Anything."

"I was wondering...sometimes I think about it...does your leg hurt you?"

Adam shot a glance at Rebecca, but her attention was on Sara.

"Nope. See, my leg is made of titanium. Tap on it. It doesn't hurt at all."

He listened hard, ready to jump in and deflect if needed. Rebecca, however, seemed very calm and matter-of-fact. Duh! She was a medic. She dealt with patients all the time, answering medical questions. He started to relax.

"Does it come off or do you sleep in it?"

Rebecca was quiet for a moment, but just as Adam was about to break in, she replied. "You already know the answer to that, Sara, but maybe you forgot. I used crutches one evening when you were at Sea View House. So what do you think?"

Sara nodded vigorously. "Yup. I forgot. I do know the answer. It comes off. But I wish...I wish...that you weren't there at the marathon." Her eyes filled. "It must have hurt..."

"No, no, sweetheart." Rebecca cupped Sara's face, brushed away her tears. "I promise you, I didn't feel a thing. I was knocked to the pavement, but lots of people helped me. Why, one woman took off her belt, and an EMT used it as a tourniquet for me. Do you know what a tourniquet is?"

"To stop the bleeding."

"Right, smart girl! After that, I was put in an ambulance and whisked away to the hospital. I had so many helpers, I wasn't afraid at all."

Adam wondered if Bart had introduced her to the Blarney Stone. A great way to tell Sara, but he knew there was a much bigger story behind her words. "I think that's enough for today, Sara."

"But you said if I want to know something, I should ask questions."

"And use some judgment."

Rebecca cut in. "You can ask me anything you want to, Sara. Anything at all."

"Okay. Wanna do manicures after dinner? It'll be more fun with a girl who's neater than Katie."

From the sublime to the ridiculous, but on much safer ground. Safer still would be general conversation around the picnic table outside. "Steak's ready," he called. "Let's eat!"

#

Safe? Maybe not. Not while Rebecca was throwing out a dozen ideas to "rescue" his rescue center.

"We need a fundraiser," she said, her fork pointing his way. "And for that, we need help. Allies. Friends…the whole town."

Her eyes glowed like moonlight, her words barely registering as he stared at her. So animated—on his behalf. He could watch her forever but forced himself to tune back in. He'd heard enough to feel flattered. The woman had done a lot of thinking about his greyhound rescue center. Which had to mean she cared. But a fundraiser? A big event? He was used to sitting at his computer, writing proposals to funding agencies. Not coordinating an event.

"We?" he asked. "Are you the first volunteer?"

"The ROMEOs. That's who we need. They'll know how to make some noise, promote it, and get a crowd together."

Interesting. The last time she'd been part of a crowd, he'd had to help her escape. "Not gonna run away this time?"

Her brow furrowed, then cleared. "Ahh—I remember. But no, I won't run away as long as you don't."

Now he was truly confused. "Why would I?"

"Well, you don't like the limelight, either, but more important"—she leaned toward him across the table—"in my humble opinion, this fundraiser can't be just about the greys. The agency that turned you down had a point. Pilgrim Cove is too small. Greyhounds are too specialized. If you want a rescue center, I think it's got to be for all dogs—greyhounds, other breeds, and the ever popular no-breed-at-all doggie."

"And cats, too," said Sara. "We saved Butterscotch, and look at him now, all grown up and happy. And bossy."

Little pitchers had big ears. But his daughter also had the cutest grin with her mom's dimple and sparkling dark eyes. The child knew how to make her point. When Sara and Rebecca high-fived each other, he knew he had to take charge. If he called for a vote right then, he'd lose.

His mind raced. He'd been so focused on returning the retired greyhounds to good health and finding good homes, he hadn't considered alternatives. He loved all dogs, but those gentle giants had a special place in his heart. They were a part of him. He'd grown up with them, couldn't remember a time in his life without them. They'd been more than pets to an only child. They'd been his friends. How could he let them down when they needed help so badly at the end of their racing careers?

Standing now, he started to pace. There had always been a lot more funding for general animal shelters than for the greys by themselves. And he couldn't do everything!

Suddenly, Rebecca was beside him, her hands reaching for his. "It's about numbers, Adam."

Of course it was. He'd get a lot more support catering to all animals than if he stuck only to the greys. "Maybe we'll get lucky," he said. "Maybe someone in town will win the lottery and donate a chunk of money to the rescue center. A financial angel who loves animals."

Their fingers intertwined, and he looked down into her dark eyes. "But that angel won't be prettier than you." He kissed her gently. And wanted more. "If my daughter weren't here…" he whispered, loving the rosy color that stained her cheeks. Using willpower he didn't know he had, he stopped himself from exploring deeper. He could still tell Sara she'd seen only a kiss between friends. He had to make more private time for him and Becca.

"And you'd still take in some racers," she whispered, sticking to the safer topic.

He answered her with another kiss.

Until Sara broke in. "But what are we going to do?" she said in exasperation. "How will we get everyone together?"

Becca stepped away from him, a smile flashing across her face. "I've got that covered," she said. "A race. Right on the beach. What could be more appropriate?"

"A race for the rescues," said Adam. "A great idea. We can do a 5K. Walk or run. That's a good distance for everyone—adults, kids, teens…and as a bonus, they can do it with or without their hounds. All dogs welcome."

He could just picture the race scene in the early morning, people swarming the beach, tents set up, water jugs, dogs…tee shirts.

"It would be a perfect time to make a comeback," said Rebecca. "I'm as strong as I'll ever be thanks to all my therapy. I wish I could consider a 5K."

He pictured Rebecca taking a spill, the sand invading her prosthesis. He winced. Nope. Not gonna happen. "One day you will," he said. "After you get the special leg with the running foot. For now you'll be busy with me registering people, collecting money, and all that stuff."

She stroked his cheek. "I think, Adam, we both need a financial angel."

CHAPTER TEN

"You're crazy about him, aren't you?"

On Saturday, a week after the dinner at Adam's house, Becca stood at her kitchen sink, loading the dishwasher with the dirty plates her mother had brought in from outside. She knew her mom well enough to know that Angela had more to say. Words to squash the hope and love Becca held in her heart. Normally, she kept her mouth shut. Today, a fire stirred inside her. Her mom was right. She was crazy about Adam.

"Just be careful, Rebecca. I didn't raise a dummy, did I?"

"Your rosy outlook is so encouraging." Becca's sarcastic auto-response was her usual fallback, but the sarcasm never worked.

Her mom stepped back, looking hurt.

"All right. I'm sorry I spoke that way," Rebecca said, "but can't you ever view the bright side of life? Why do you still see the worst?"

"No, no honey. In you, I see the best. And when I think what you've gone through…and how much progress you've made, I'm so proud."

Her mom's arms tightened around her, and Becca felt her defenses evaporate. She and Angela had their differences, but she loved her mother. She'd been a steadying presence—after her early debacle with the creep so long ago.

"Proud? Because 'life hurts and I'm dealing with it'?"

"At least you'll survive. And that's the most important thing."

Angela had a point, but... "But I want more than that, Mom. I want a full life. Adam is...wonderful. And yes, I'm crazy about him. I never expected to meet anyone, especially right now. I thought I'd hide out here until Josie found a place for us." She glanced toward the patio. "But then Adam...and Sara too..."

"Well, I suppose dreams are for the young," Angela said with a sigh. "And Adam seems like a nice enough young man. Just be careful. Don't jump."

Careful. Careful. Careful. Another code word. Her mother carried a lifetime of regret for an early mistake. Her judgment was off. "Stop beating yourself up," said Rebecca. "The creep took advantage of you."

Her mother nodded. "But I let him," she said, her voice hoarse. "Like a weasel, he stole your father's life insurance money from me. Sweet talk, big talk. Oh, I was so weak when I should have been strong—for both our sakes. I was frightened of being on my own with a child to raise. I was lonely, too." She stroked Becca's cheek. "I'm still lonely and older now as well. I don't want the same for you."

What was her point? That Adam would take advantage of her and leave her in the dirt? "Adam's not a creep. Far from it."

Angela wrung her hands over one another. Becca recognized the nervous habit tinged with guilt. She used to call it her mom's Lady Macbeth mode.

"Didn't I say Adam seems like a nice guy?" Angela continued. "But...they all seem wonderful in the beginning." Her glance roved around the room, avoiding Becca's gaze. "I know I can't advise you what to do anymore. You're an adult. And everything I say is suspect. If I say to move ahead with Adam, you'll think it's to avoid being lonely. If I tell you to be cautious, you'll think it's because I trust no one."

Becca smiled. "And I'd be about right."

The kitchen door swung open. Adam and Sara filled the space with their laughter and more dirty dishes.

"Just got a call from Bart Quinn," said Adam. "All the permissions and permits from the town are in order for the race."

The idea of Race for the Rescues had lit a fuse under the ROMEOs. Almost all were pet parents, and they'd latched on to the fundraiser in a heartbeat.

"I'm glad we've already lined up some publicity." Becca turned to her mother. "We've got spots reserved for public service announcements on local radio stations and posters for every storefront in town and the next town over."

"I'll be handing out fliers to every patient who comes into the office," said Adam, "and leaving fliers with all the stores on Main Street."

"I'm helping, too. I'm telling all my friends at day camp about it," added Sara. "They all want to run. And you know what else I did?"

"What?" asked Becca. The child looked like she'd swallowed a terrific secret.

"I made a list of ten reasons to have a cat or dog, so my friends could talk their parents into adopting a pet. I figured if they could make a good argument, instead of just whining, they'd win. And we'd win. We need forever homes, you know."

Becca reached for Sara, held her tight, and kissed her on the temple. She couldn't help herself. "You are amazing, kiddo. So smart. So clever." The girl's return hug was just as tight, trusting and satisfying. Becca almost cried. Keeping her arms around Sara, she moved her head to search for Adam but caught such a pained look on her mother's face, she gasped. "What's wrong, Mom?"

Angela swallowed, transferred her gaze slightly from Adam's daughter to her own. "This child is you. I see you. Whipcord smart. Pretty dark curls. Only one parent to depend on. But I never let you have a dog. I was trying to pay the rent. I'm sorry."

More regrets. What was going on here? Why today? "I'm thirty years old, Mom, and in the end, I survived just fine without a dog."

Angela sighed a huge sigh. "And you're still trying to survive despite everything. I guess I taught you right."

An image of Bart Quinn shaking his head flashed through Becca's mind. She hid a smile. "Life can hurt, Mom, but it can also hold joy. I'd rather reach for the joy."

"Thank God," murmured Adam.

"I see that," Angela replied quietly at the same time. "But it's very risky business."

"You know what's riskier?" asked Adam, his glance switching between the two women and then answering his own question. "Forgetting about dessert!"

Becca laughed, her tension relieved. The man knew exactly what he was doing.

#

Sitting at the edge of her bed already wearing pajamas, Becca could hear her mother opening and closing closet doors in the kitchen. How could she be hungry when they'd had a full dinner including a heavenly Mississippi mud pie? Chocolate to die for.

She grabbed her crutches and made her way down the hall, Ginger a silent shadow. Her mother had a mug on the counter and was searching the pantry. "Tea bags are on the middle shelf."

Angela swirled. "Hi, honey. Did I wake you? I tried to be quiet."

"I hadn't gone to bed yet. Neither had Ginger."

"I don't know much about dogs," said Angela, filling her cup and placing it in the microwave, "but I think she loves you."

Becca smiled. "Yeah, well, I love her, too."

Her mom's thoughtful expression almost made Becca squirm. "Oh, sweetheart…" Her voice trailed off.

Ginger wasn't forever. That's what her mom meant. Maybe so, but Becca had chosen to live each day in the present. Ginger was part of her now.

"I'm glad you've joined me," Angela said, starting anew. "Midnight talks are the best."

For whom? Becca wondered.

"Here, let me help you," said Angela, pushing a chair away from the table, making more room for Becca to maneuver.

"I'm fine, Mom. I don't need help. I like using the stool in here anyway." She sat at her usual place in front of the counter and faced her mother.

"What's on your mind, Mom?"

"I'll say it straight out." The microwave dinged, and she took her cup of hot tea to the table. "That nice young man of yours needs money. That's why you're knocking yourself out with this race of his. Don't do it, Becca. Don't give him any of your savings or your award. You've known him only for a short time. You're not married to him…"

"Whoa. Stop! Just stop and calm down. If you weren't so upset, Mom, I'd laugh. Think about what you said. What award? What money? My savings are small. And Adam knows that. In fact, he gave me a job. He didn't have to do that."

Her mother looked at her with pity in her eyes. She reached for her hand. "Becca…are you living under a rock? Do you not listen to the news or speak with your friends who were hurt?"

"I'm on an email loop with them. Of course I keep up. I know there's talk of some compensation, but that's all it is. Talk. And even if it's true, it can't be much. It's all voluntary donations."

Angela closed her eyes and shook her head. "I can't believe this," she murmured. Leaning toward Becca, she said, "We live in the most generous country in the world. Americans have big hearts. The One Fund Boston account is growing every day. That's the talk in the city, in the newspapers. Especially the Boston papers. And it's more than rumor. Attorney Kenneth Feinberg will decide the amounts. He's the man who handled the 9/11 awards."

Her mother took a deep breath. "Now do you believe me? So, when you get your share, don't you give any of it away. Not to Adam. Not to anyone. You'll need it in the future."

Her mom had said a mouthful about awards, but Becca's heart was heavy with her implication. "You don't think I'll ever work again," she whispered. "You don't think I'll be able to support myself." Working hard to overcome her physical disabilities was easier than dealing with this. Her own mother didn't believe in her.

"I didn't say that."

But she understood what Angela omitted. Neither of them really knew how high Becca's medical expenses would be in the future. Her disability insurance was temporary. Sea View House was temporary. Real life was waiting just around the corner.

Her mom took her hands and squeezed. "I can offer you a home, honey. You're welcome to live with me. No matter what."

#

Never! Her mother's invitation stung. Sure, she might have meant well, offering reassurance, but living in rural Massachusetts would cut down Becca's options. Would make her more housebound than she'd ever want to be. She'd rather go it alone in Beantown than go back to country life. Even Pilgrim Cove was a better choice. The town might be small, but a thirty-minute ferry ride was all she'd need to get to the city. Small was different from rural.

Becca waved her mom good-bye on Monday morning, after exchanging hard hugs. Angela had a long ride across the entire state ahead of her.

"A weekend isn't enough," said Becca.

"Be glad I added today. It's all I could afford. Remember, I used up vacation time after the accident."

Very true. "Well, if I do get any money, you can take a week off without pay. I'll pay!" One last kiss and her mom drove out of Pilgrim Cove. Becca watched the car disappear from sight and, with a sigh, slid into her own car with Ginger and drove to the clinic.

Adam met her at the door. "How was yesterday?"

"She's a mother. She worries."

He shrugged. "So what's new? She'll come around the more she visits."

She squeezed his hand. "I don't need her approval. My decisions are my own."

His eyes lit up; his smile could have warmed the whole hospital. "That's what I hoped. I know I didn't rate an A with her."

"No one would have. No man, anyway." She tilted her head back and looked up. "I'd say you earned a B-plus. Not too shabby for a first timer."

His eyes widened. "First timer? You're not sixteen."

"First timer since the explosion. The calendar starts anew."

"But you're still you."

He got her. He understood. She brushed his nose featherlight with her finger. "That's the truth, Adam."

His embrace lifted all woes. Right there in the clinic, in the reception area, where anyone could have seen, except it was just a bit too early for patients. With his kiss, those woes disappeared into the ether as though they'd never been. He hadn't used the word, but she could feel the love, the caring, the sweetness.

He whispered in her ear. "How about a date this Wednesday? Something special. No kids. No dogs. Sara has an overnight at camp."

Her heart raced and she nodded against his chest. Wednesday could be very special.

#

Later that morning, in between sterilizing instruments and answering the phone, Becca looked up to see Arlene Farr walk into the clinic. Becca's stomach tightened as she immediately understood her time at Adam's office was coming to an end.

"I brought my mom home with me," Arlene said after greeting Becca and chatting about the clinic. "She's doing much better but can't be left alone all day. I'm wondering if we can split the shift between us. Mornings for you and afternoons for me."

Her job had been temporary, and she'd known that from the get-go. The dose of reality, however, made her smile feel pasted on. "I have therapy two afternoons a week, so that works out perfectly."

"That's wonderful. Thank you so much, Rebecca. I need mornings to get my mother up, dressed, fed, and settled before I can leave her. I guess I was worried for nothing."

Becca's smile came more naturally now, and she felt herself relax. Arlene was a lovely person with mother problems of a different sort. "No reason to worry. It was never my job to keep." But she'd happily pounce on the reprieve.

Arlene's eyes sparkled. "A little birdie told me you could wind up with a better…hmm…position….around here."

Her meaning was clear. *Keep your cool, Becca, just keep your cool.* "Seems the Pilgrim Cove rumor mill is spinning in the wrong direction."

"Whatever you say." Arlene chuckled and, with a wave, left the clinic. "I'll start back here tomorrow."

Rebecca tracked the woman as she left the office. Tomorrow meant the beginning of change. Soon Arlene would be back full time—as she should be. As for Becca? A job search in Boston now headed her to-do list and brought an ache to her heart.

CHAPTER ELEVEN

He wanted to wine her, dine her, and make love to her. He wanted to sweep her off her feet…but not in the literal sense. He didn't want to scare her, so he'd been playing it cool. At least he thought so. He'd been treating Rebecca with respect and following her lead before taking over. Their kisses left him hungry for more. Definitely more. And he thought she reacted the same way.

Rebecca was different from Lila. Different from Eileen. She was uniquely herself. His love for her was growing every day. But…well, commitment made him nervous. An honest assessment. What if she walked out like Lila had? What if something more dire happened to her like it had to Eileen?

He looked in the bathroom mirror and slapped his cologne on harder than necessary. Idiot! Nothing bad was going to happen. Just the opposite. He'd planned a fabulous evening for them. A romantic evening. They definitely needed some time alone.

He grabbed his wallet and keys and spotted Butterscotch lying on top of the fridge. "Watch the place, pal. You're on your own."

A mighty yawn was the big boy's only response, and Adam saluted. The house seemed abnormally quiet. No dogs since he'd delivered Honey and Duke to their new home with the Levines. Ginger now lived with Rebecca, and no one had suggested she return to his house. Not even Sara. Becca and the grey seemed happy with each other. He wondered if their meeting had been well-timed serendipity or a bit of Bart's magic. No question, the two provided some comfort and therapy for each other.

With a light step, he headed out the door.

And lost his breath when Rebecca opened hers.

Smoky-looking eyes, dark waves down to her bare shoulders. Bare…smooth, silky skin. A strapless long dress in all kinds of reds and scarlets that clung and swirled at the same time. Colorful beads draped around her neck. She was a bird of paradise.

"Cat got your tongue?" she teased.

"Wow. You're beautiful."

"You're not too shabby yourself."

He'd chosen a light green dress shirt, sleeves rolled to just below the elbows, brown slacks and belt, loafers. His stuff matched. Or blended. Or something. He knew they went together.

"I ironed the shirt," he said.

Her eyes widened, a laugh emerged, and she kissed him on the cheek. "Too funny. But I like it."

She stepped back. "Mom and I shopped in town, and she treated me to the dress. Shoes, too." She swooshed the skirt aside and showed off a red leather flat. "Judging by your reaction, I think they were worth every penny." She dimpled up at him, then turned away. "Let me get my purse, and we'll be off."

He watched her efficient movements almost in a trance. *Worth every penny.* She wanted to look good—for him. The evening promised to be fantastic.

#

"Boston by boat…what a wonderful idea." Adam had mentioned a special evening and had more imagination than Rebecca. She'd ridden the ferry a number of times since arriving in Pilgrim Cove, but somehow, none of her prior trips measured up to this. On prior crossings to the rehab center, no one had held her hand or stood at the rail with her. No one had laughed and chatted with her or pointed out places of interest. No one had arranged for dinner at the Rowes Wharf Sea Grille along the Harborwalk. But Adam had that night.

At an outside terrace, they were treated to live music, a menu filled with temptation, and an unmatched view as the sun set over the harbor. Becca sat down and took her time absorbing the atmosphere.

"I thought I knew Beantown, but this is a treat."

"For both of us." He shifted back in his chair. "Sometimes, we get lost in the day-to-day responsibilities and forget to make time…"

But he'd made time for her almost since they'd met. First with his nightly visits, then swimming with his friends on their boat, and then a dinner at his house. "Some people don't smell those roses," said Becca, "but I-I don't think you're one of them."

His brow lifted; a tight smile appeared. "I'd disagree with you, but I don't want to ruin your opinion or the mood." His expression brightened. "But if you're right, then I'll give you the credit." He reached across the table for her hand. "Since you've arrived in Pilgrim Cove, everything's been…more fun."

Her breath hitched. Time stopped. He'd nailed it. "Adam…" she whispered. "For me, too. It's been amazing and so unexpected." Fun was the furthest thing from her mind when she'd arrived at Sea View House. So much had changed in five weeks.

His hand tightened on hers. He leaned over the table and kissed her on the mouth. Right there. In front of everyone. Who cared?

She returned the pressure and felt her heart race. The evening had just begun. So much more to look forward to.

A glass of wine, a cup of chowder, and a jumbo shrimp cocktail were enough for Becca. But Adam downed a portion of roasted duck, feeding her a forkful every time she patted her tummy and sighed. Finally, she held up her hand. "Enough! One more bite and you'll have to roll me home."

"Sorry," he said. "No can do."

Confused now, she paid full attention.

"Didn't bring the wheelchair."

She startled for a moment, but his hazel eyes twinkled with warmth and humor, and she started to laugh. And then she laughed until she cried. Like a plug pulled from the dyke. "Oh, my God," she said, wiping tears from her cheeks. "You got me. You really got me. And messed up my mascara, too."

Surely, making love couldn't be more intimate than joking about a horrible event she'd have to live with for the rest of her life.

"Sweetheart, I learned the hard way. If you don't laugh again, you'll cry. And we can't have that."

The waiter cleared their table and flourished a dessert menu.

"Not another bite," said Rebecca. "I'll burst."

"Just bring me the bill," said Adam, glancing at their server.

The man coughed. "No, sir. By order of the proprietor, your meals are on the house."

"Excuse me?"

The man nodded at Rebecca, then waved to someone else. "Here's the owner. It's been an honor to serve you."

With his hand outstretched to Adam and then to Becca, the newcomer wasted no words. "Ms. Hart, you will never pay for a meal here, and I hope you return many times." He looked at Adam. "She's already paid, and we take care of our own. Our heroes."

She felt the heat rise. Her face flamed. "I'm no hero."

Adam put a twenty on the table. "The server did a good job."

The man picked it up. "We'll donate it to the One Fund Boston. And now, I'll say good night. But stay as long as you want. Enjoy, enjoy."

Becca remained frozen to her chair. Adam walked around the table to her, leaned down, and kissed her cheek. "I'm sorry you were embarrassed. Wanna blow this joint?" he asked in a bad gangster imitation.

Suddenly light-headed, she leaned back and briefly closed her eyes.

"How about a walk along the harbor before our ferry ride back?"

She offered a shaky smile. "A short walk sounds perfect. And then home to Pilgrim Cove." Her safety. Her hideaway.

"You got it."

She had the strength and stamina for more than a short walk but had never tested herself for distance. "I've changed my mind. Let's just walk until we don't want to anymore. And let's forget what happened in the restaurant."

Holding hands with Adam on a moonlit summer night, their fingers intertwined, walking along the harbor, seeing boats bobbing in their moorings, watching the parade of people…all happening in downtown Boston. Her adopted city. With the distractions they provided, she put the restaurant incident behind her. Until…

"Oh, my God! Look at that, Adam." She pointed to signs hanging in a row of shop windows: Boston Strong.

"That's you," said Adam. "That's us. That's an entire nation. Everyone became a Bostonian the day of the marathon." His hand pressed hers a bit harder. "It's a fact, Rebecca. You need to face it. Whether you want it or not, the spotlight is on you and the others."

She hadn't paid attention to the news. Her mother was right. Becca had been living under a rock. But now she had to crawl out and understand the bigger picture. She took a deep breath. Tomorrow would be soon enough. Tonight belonged to Adam.

#

A cool breeze engulfed them on the ride back, but with Adam's arm around her, Becca had no complaints about the weather. They stood at the rail and watched Pilgrim Cove's small harbor come into view, growing larger as the minutes passed. Was it her imagination, or was the town welcoming her home? Maybe her heart spoke. Maybe she was still surprised at what had happened at the Sea Grille. Maybe she was growing to love the place…and the people in it. Or maybe her warm feelings were generated by one special person, the one standing next to her.

Of course, he kissed her at the door. Of course, she wanted another taste. Dessert was a good excuse, only an excuse, to invite him inside. They both knew it and bypassed the kitchen and dog. Step by slow step, as if a choreographed dance, they made their way down the hall to her bedroom, their mouths clinging. His kiss was deep, hungry, his tongue darting, playing. She responded, her own hunger as strong as his.

Adam…who'd never judged. Adam…who cheered her. Who believed in her. Adam, with a sense of humor that tickled her funny bone. Adam, who made her feel whole. And safe.

She stroked his face and skimmed her fingers along his ear, his neck, anywhere she could reach. Her breasts swelled, the nipples tingling against the weave of his shirt. She moved with him across the threshold, her breath coming in gasps. She saw his flushed skin, his hazel eyes dark and hot…hot for her. And she wanted him.

His hands skimmed down her back to her waist, tightening, drawing her closer—as if that were possible—

"Come with me," Becca whispered, leading him toward the bed.

"I want to see you." His hoarse voice told its own story—a different story—but she had to ask. "My leg?"

He didn't reply. She paused, turned back. His eyes were dark with desire. His fingertips traveled across her bare shoulders, across her skin to the elastic of her strapless dress, and she savored the touch.

"So beautiful…" His mouth replaced his hands along her neckline, his kisses making her dizzy. She reached for him, clung to him, and somehow, her dress was gone, a folded pile of material on the floor. Maybe he hadn't heard her question. "But what about…?

"It doesn't matter. We'll get to it later, whenever…. You're beautiful and perfect."

Love words. To her ears. She stood tall, unbuttoning his shirt. She could have prolonged the act into a titillating fandango but wanted him next to her, body to body. Her legs wobbled as desire built. "Ohh..."

"I'll finish this. You do that." Adam's jaw jerked toward her leg.

Without thinking twice, she sat on the bed, broke the suction, and placed the titanium in its usual spot, barely taking her eyes from him. His shirt joined her dress on the floor; his unbuckled belt allowed his slacks to fall, too. She lay back on the pillows, arms up and out, the desire on his face almost more than she could bear.

"Gorgeous, sexy...you're incredible," he whispered.

More love words...beautiful love words.

He lowered himself over her, slowly coming closer. Her arms tightened around him, pulling him down. His kisses covered her everywhere. On her neck, breasts, and nipples. Her body tingled all over and she moaned. He entered carefully and with an ease that surprised her. But his taut face, his quivering muscles revealed the caution he took, the effort he made. For her sake.

She tightened her thighs around him, and he broke. Caution flew out the window. They locked and rocked. A floodtide of pleasure enveloped her, like waves crashing on the shore over and over in the rhythm as ancient as the ocean itself.

After the last crash came—all too soon—and they lay exhausted together, Adam propped himself on his elbow and smiled down at her. His eyes gleamed with that mischievous spark she loved. "Was it good for you, too?" he asked.

She laughed and replied between gasps. "Is that all you can say? So unoriginal, I'm disappointed."

But he began to laugh, too, and she wasn't sure what he was thinking anymore. "Okay, okay. I almost hate to ask what your goofy grin means..."

He kissed her again and said, "There *is* an upside after all. Easy access works well."

She understood instantly. "Point taken. I totally agree."

CHAPTER TWELVE

A call she hadn't expected came in on her cell phone the next afternoon among the flurry of others she received about the Race for the Rescues. Although Adam's name garnered the attention and his signature was required on paperwork, Becca had become the point person for the event. Working only mornings in the clinic allowed her time to help. Between coordinating the ROMEOs' assignments and accomplishments, creating promotions, and fielding questions from the general public all over eastern New England, Becca was busier than an army of worker bees.

So when she saw a Boston area code in her readout, she automatically answered. She would have connected with any area code at that point. Every call was a potential race participant, a potential donor.

"Good afternoon. Race for the Rescues. Rebecca speaking." And then she listened. She listened to the representative of One Fund Boston who spoke on behalf of Attorney Kenneth Feinberg, who was charged with deciding the amount of the awards, just like he'd done with other big cases.

"Awards? Are you saying I'm to receive a financial award?" asked Rebecca.

"Yes, Ms. Hart. That's exactly what we're saying."

It seemed her mother had been right. Some kind of settlement would be made. In the beginning, she'd figured on a few thousand dollars, maybe a bit more. She now wished Angela was with her to confirm what she was hearing from the official.

The amount stunned her. "But-but…are you sure? That's—that's really a lot of money." *A lot* was an understatement. One million, two hundred thousand dollars. She couldn't wrap her mind around it.

"Over sixty million dollars was collected specifically for the victims of the attack. In the beginning, we didn't realize the donations would be so generous. We were hoping to give a million to the double amputees, but the money poured in, and we're happy to make these awards. We hope it will make life easier."

"Oh."

"It's a lump sum, tax-free payment regardless of your income or medical costs. You also have not relinquished your right to sue."

Sue? That would be ridiculous. Who would she sue? Would a lawsuit bring her leg back? "Uh…thank you. Thank you very much. I'm a little overwhelmed right now."

"Just one more thing you should know."

"Yes?"

"The specifics of the awards will be in the newspapers tomorrow. So you might get calls from local reporters…"

Great. "Long-lost relatives, too, I suppose?"

"Hopefully not. Well, good luck to you. You'll get a call from Mr. Steinberg himself, as well. And we'll be in touch if any more monies come in."

Becca leaned back in her chair and just breathed. Funny how even good news could be hard to absorb after such a long time adjusting to "making the best" of her new normal. How long, really, had it been? She glanced at the calendar on the counter. What seemed like forever was less than three months. Long enough to accept her disability. Long enough to meet a wonderful man. Long enough to fall in love. Adam! He'd be so happy for her. And the rehab staff! As her brain snapped into gear, she picked up the phone and first called her team in Boston. Adam would have to wait another minute.

"I need an appointment with the Prosthetics Department." Her new normal had become a better normal. Money might not buy happiness, but it could buy her some freedom. Freedom to swim in the ocean and shower standing up. Freedom to run a 5K or a 10K, or a half marathon…or next year's Boston Marathon. With an appropriate and properly fitted leg, anything was possible. Anything.

As she waited to be connected, her heart began to pound. She felt hot one moment and cold the next. Her world had changed in an instant. The knowledge drenched her to the core like playful ocean waves pulling her under water and then setting her free. She now had the means to do anything. She could have legs that matched so closely no one but an expert could tell the difference. And she could wear high heels with a specially designed foot. Two and a half inches high. She loved the idea.

Maybe she was a shallow person. She was grateful to be alive, of course she was, but now she wanted more. She wanted to enjoy being a girl. Was that normal? Should she feel guilty?

Over a million dollars. That was certainly a lot of money. Moola. Bucks. Gelt. Greenbacks. Shekels. Cold cash. She had to be careful with it. Prosthetics would need repairs or eventually wear out. The award had to last a lifetime.

#

"As soon as the news hit, the phone rang," said Rebecca, popping a slice of pizza into her mouth.

"Uh-oh," said Adam. "You don't look happy, but you sure look cute with the sauce on your chin."

He and Sara were at Sea View House. The workweek was over, the weekend just starting, which meant more time to devote to the Race for the Rescues. He grabbed a napkin and wiped away the errant sauce that had somehow worked its way to her cheek.

"It's not like I won the state lottery or something," continued Becca, on a roll. "I may not know a damn thing about investments, but these people are unbelievable. They're vultures."

"Yup. Sharks."

"So I'm just putting it all in the bank. Where it's safe."

"Good idea," concurred Adam. "When in doubt, do nothing." He'd not become a target for her crosshairs, that's for sure. And money could be a delicate subject that he, for one, was not going to touch. Not even to tell her that her painfully won capital would hardly grow in a traditional savings account. Nope, he wasn't that brave, not when she sizzled and flamed, her arms gesturing, her face a kaleidoscope of expressions and emotion as she ranted about so-called investment brokers.

"You've got enough energy to spare tonight," he said. "How about we take the hound and head toward the shore—a walk along the water's edge."

She stopped in mid-gesture, on her feet almost before he finished speaking. "Yes! I have a pedometer, and I want to see how far I can go. Thanks, Adam." She kissed him then, right in front of Sara, who watched with great interest.

Becca's joy was contagious. Without thinking twice, he stood up, wrapped her in his arms, and slowly twirled around. He loved the feel of her against him. He loved holding her, kissing her. And hearing her squeal with surprise as she turned.

When he set her down, she automatically regained her balance. "Nice, Rebecca. Very nice," he said. "You'll be ready for a surfboard in no time."

She eyed him with a challenge. "Definitely. With my aqua limb."

He did a double take. He'd been kidding, but it seemed she had big plans.

"Daddy!" interrupted Sara. "Don't you know that Ms. Rebecca can do anything? She's the bravest lady I ever saw."

His breath hitched; his chest ached. Sara had been too young to appreciate Eileen's courage. "We both knew another lady who was very brave."

Sara stood still, her brow furrowed, while Rebecca's profound silence rang in his ears. He locked on to his daughter.

"Mommy," she whispered. "You mean Mommy."

He heard Becca's, "Ohh, sweetheart…"

"That's right, honey. Your mom and Ms. Rebecca are the best and the bravest."

"Especially your mom…" said Becca.

She didn't have to be modest. Not for his sake. Or Sara's. Each woman was special in her own right. But he and Sara needed to talk privately. She shouldn't read anything into Becca's kisses and friendliness. He wasn't sure about their relationship now and how it would end. With her financial windfall, the ground beneath Adam suddenly felt shaky. Money changed people. Becca now had more options to lead a fully independent life, maybe go back to her old life. Perhaps to her old job that she loved. Maybe a small-town vet wouldn't be enough for her. Maybe the hustle and bustle of Boston were more appealing. That was an awful lot of maybes.

They'd enjoyed a wonderful night together. No doubt about being in synch with a tenderness and playfulness that amazed him. Delighted him. But that was no guaranty for the future. Maybe he was heading for a third strike.

He glanced at the courageous woman in the room. Would she vanish like his appetite just had? A good relationship had to be based on honesty. Right now, however, he had to be honest with himself and not assume anything. She needed time and space to figure out the million-dollar element in her life.

#

She could see Adam was troubled. As they walked along the shore, he became distracted and absent-minded. It seemed to Becca that he appeared uneasy whenever Eileen's name came up as it had done in the house. If that was the case, then they needed to clear the air. He had to understand that Becca was not a carbon copy of his deceased wife. Nor was she a substitute.

"Something wrong?" she asked.

"Ginger's after every gull," said Adam. "Good thing the leash is strong."

"Good thing your arm is strong!" Superficial conversation. She'd given him an opening and he hadn't taken it. She'd follow his lead—for now.

"We should have gone to the soccer field, where I can let her go free. It's fenced."

Becca understood by now that Ginger couldn't be counted on to come at Adam's call. Her instinct was to chase and run. A strong instinct of sighthounds. Becca had read up about the breed on the Net and had browsed some books in Adam's clinic.

"I've got a ball," added Sara. "She could chase that at the field."

"Well, then," said Becca, "why don't you guys take Ginger over there and give her a good time. I'm about ready to call it a day myself." And if that didn't provide a graceful way to cut the evening short, she didn't know what would.

"Oh, no, Ms. Rebecca. You come, too."

The child's invitation came from the heart. Becca embraced her and held her close. "I'll see you tomorrow morning at the Race committee meeting. You're a very important member of the group. It wouldn't feel right without you."

Sea View House had become the committee's meeting place because of the beach behind it, where registration tables would be set up, water bottles distributed, and monies collected, too. About a dozen people would be gathering in the morning to plan.

They had retraced their steps and were almost at the yard now. Evening shadows surrounded them.

"Want me to keep Ginger overnight?" asked Adam. "So we won't disturb you later after she's had her run?"

Her mouth tightened. So did her stomach. Ginger had become her roommate. Her friend. The thought of her absence made Becca's heart sink. More important, however, was that Adam raised the question at all. Was this the first step in cooling their relationship? She definitely thought their evening together meant something; she could have sworn Adam felt the same.

"Since when are you concerned about disturbing me?" She cocked her head. "I'd need all my fingers to count the times you've caught me sleeping on the back porch. But I understand if you want an early night yourself. You need to be sharp in the morning."

His jaw set, his back straightened, and his shoulders squared. "What I need," he said, gazing right at her, "is to figure out how to be two people at the same time. Be in two places at the same time. And read two minds at the same time. Oh…and find the right words for each one of me." He pointed a finger at Becca. "See you in the morning because she"—he inclined his head toward Sara—"will have to go to bed…. Get it?"

"Got it," Becca whispered.

"Good."

#

The iced tea was almost gone. The lemonade was almost gone. According to Bart Quinn, a lot of talking made people thirsty. But there were still some cookies, he pointed out, because the man had brought dozens. As had Adam.

Becca slipped into the group with ease. Her role as an organizer had something to do with it, but as each person entered the house, she realized she knew every one of them now. Peggy from work, Doc Rosen and his wife, Marsha, Rachel and Jack Levine, Rick O'Brien and Dee, Jason Parker with Katie and baby Rosemary, who was now a month old. Lila was covering the real estate office for the morning. Laura Parker, a key event planner, showed up with her stepsons, Casey and Brian.

All ages. Everyone talking. A million ideas were thrown around at once. Becca loved it.

"The promo and posters are up and out. The PSAs are scheduled. So now we need to concentrate on the logistics of the day," said Adam.

"I guess that's my bailiwick," said Laura. "Marsha and I are cancer survivors and have worked on other races. We can do it again for this one. For the sake of my rescued cat, Midnight." She winked at the boys.

"I'll help with the setup, too," offered Rebecca.

"You should focus on the publicity," said Laura. "Promo can't stop until after the event, when you'll publicize the grand result. Give folks a feeling of satisfaction. Their contributions mattered."

Fine with Becca. She was a team player…most of the time. At least, she was at work. She could be a team player here, too. She happened to glance at Sara and was surprised to see her shaking her head. "What's wrong, Sara?"

"So far the race is only people," said Sara. "I think everybody needs to see some pets. We need a parade, a dog parade. You know how I love parades."

"Great idea! But we'll also need cats," said Casey. "Mom rescued Midnight, and she's just as important as any old dog."

"Well, if Midnight is in the parade, then Butterscotch is in it, too!" said Sara. "Right, Dad?"

Becca grabbed her cell and snapped Adam's picture. If he could see the anguish on his face… The man was drowning.

Adam looked at the kids, then at Chief O'Brien. "Can we get the soccer field for after the race?"

"And we can have prizes," said Sara, clearly excited and not waiting for the chief to reply. "The first prize can be a free visit to the clinic or a free heartworm shot. Right, Dad?"

An awful lot of "Right, Dad's?" were being thrown at him, but Becca gave Adam credit for holding on. The man simply could not say no to his daughter. She had to admit, however, that in the time she'd known Sara, the child didn't ask for much. Once again, the girl reminded Becca of herself years ago. She, too, had learned quickly what was allowed and what was futile. She'd learned about money and that her mother's first reaction to any request was to say no. Sara's environment and hers may have been different, but figuring out a parent was the same. Especially a single parent where there was no chance to appeal to a more sympathetic authority.

"Here's the deal," said Adam, looking from one child to the other. "Butterscotch and Midnight are terrific cats. They are wonderful examples of what a rescue is all about. As far as showing them off, however…that's another story. Have you ever heard of cats and dogs being in a show together? Or in a parade together?"

He got the children thinking.

"I saw a cat show on TV," said Casey. "They're in cages and some have curtains. The cages are on tables."

Adam nodded. "Each feline is taken out one at a time by its owner and raised high to where people can see them. But if we have cats and dogs together and even one kitty escapes…well…you know what can happen."

Four quiet children stared at the vet. Four sad children.

"I know," said Sara, brightening up. "This year we'll have a dog parade, and next year we'll have a cat show. That's fair."

"You're right," said Adam. "But if we don't raise the funds this year, we might not have a rescue center at all. So let's everyone stay on point and take one year at a time."

Rebecca agreed. Change was in the air. Uncertainty. A year seemed like a long way off. Too far from the present to make a commitment about dogs, cats, or…people.

#

On Monday morning, Becca wondered if they'd overdone the publicity angle. A grizzled man with a white cat in his arms entered the office.

"I heard this was a rescue place," he began. "And this here cat needs a home. She was stuck in a tree, making pitiful sounds. So, I got a ladder and got her down. Isn't she a pretty thing with her white fur and blue eyes? I gave her some tuna, but I can't keep her."

Rebecca didn't recognize the man. Not that she'd met everyone in Pilgrim Cove yet. She probably never would. The future of this feline wasn't her decision to make. She indicated a seat. "Would you mind waiting a moment while I get Dr. Fielding?"

Five minutes later, their newest addition was in an examining room with a cage waiting for her. "There's a strong chance she's deaf, not definitely, but a good chance. Her health's not too bad. She might belong to someone and just slipped outside, got scared, and ran up a tree."

"You can create a whole story."

Adam laughed. "Stories are for others. I'd rather focus on the doctoring."

Good thing because an hour later, another visitor showed up. This time a young teenage boy with a puppy in his arms. A puppy with floppy ears and big paws, maybe a lab mix. This pup would grow big.

"My mom says we can't keep him."

Becca's heart squeezed. The boy was trying not to cry, but his lips trembled. "What's your name?"

"David."

"Well, David, is your mom allergic to dogs or something?" She'd segue into the conversation with the least probable of causes.

He shook his head. "She says a dog is too expensive. She says there would be big vet bills every year with all those shots he'd need and the cost of food.

And…and…all that stuff. So she said to come here. This is a no-kill place, isn't it?"

For the very first time since getting involved with Adam's dream, Rebecca experienced the *need*, not just the *want*, for a center. A sense of urgency infused her. The committee had better be successful in raising a ton of money. But as for the boy in front of her…what could she do for him?

"Do you live in town?" she asked, playing for time and ideas.

"Nope. I live the next town over, just outside the neck."

"Could you ride a bike here?"

"Yeah…but…"

"I have a thought…" said Becca.

Hope lit David's face. Ecstasy appeared after she finished speaking to him.

"Now all we have to do is bring your puppy to Dr. Fielding." She reached for the pup. "Come on, sweet boy. You're coming with me now." She cuddled the adorable prize and brought him to the back, into the treatment area of the clinic.

"Good timing for me," said Becca. "You're done with Mistletoe's surgery."

"Yeah. We bought the old girl some time," said Adam. "But it's not infinite. No way around that. I'll have a quiet talk with her owner." A deep sigh emanated from him.

Becca looked closer. Faint lines showed around his eyes. The brackets around his mouth were white. Every medical practice involved life-and-death issues. Adam felt his patients' pain. She patted his arm. "I'm sorry."

"And whose pup is that?" he asked, seeming to look for a distraction. "Do we have a new patient in the family?"

"Well…in a way." She quickly explained about the boy in the waiting room. "And I suggested that if he volunteered in the new rescue center every Saturday after it opened, you'd provide free medical care for this cute little pup."

The vet's eyes widened. "You did what?"

Uh-oh. "Well, what else could I do? David was so upset. He could have been Brian Parker or even your Sara with how he loves that puppy."

Adam put his hand on her shoulder. "Listen up. A veterinary practice is a business. A rescue center is a business, too, even though a lot of volunteers work there. The idea is to place the animals in a home that wants them. A home that can afford them. I'm just the conduit, sweetheart, the middleman. I'm not the financier."

But I could help this boy.

The thought brought great satisfaction. "I'm sorry, Adam. I understand where you're coming from. I really do. So don't worry about David. I'll take care of it."

His eyes narrowed, and he pursed his lips. "How?"

"I'm a"—*cough, cough*—"millionaire, aren't I? I'll take care of the charges." She waved and returned to the reception area. But not before she heard him say, "Like hell you will."

CHAPTER THIRTEEN

The commute to Boston by ferry had become routine—
almost. Rebecca stood at the rail of the boat watching
Pilgrim Cove emerge from the mist. The threat of rain
didn't bother her. Nothing bothered her today.

As soon as she was ashore, she checked the time
and headed toward Adam's house. A surprise visit.

Sara came to the door, her face lighting up when
she saw Becca. "Dad's in his office on the phone. Want
to have supper with us?" She led Becca into the kitchen.

"Let's wait for your dad." The oven timer started
ringing. Sara silenced it, opened the door, and reached
for the potholders. "It's fish," she said, wrinkling her
nose. "I could eat hotdogs and hamburgers every day,
but…no-o…we can't have so much red meat."

The child imitated Adam's inflection to a tee. Becca
covered her mouth. Openly laughing at Sara's attitude—
so typical of ten-year-olds—would not go over well.

After placing the pan on the counter, Sara pointed
to a pot on top of the stove. "Spaghetti. I think it must be
done. I'll get Dad. I'm not supposed to handle that."

"Wise girl. But you don't have to bother your dad. I can handle this."

"We gotta heat up the sauce, too…"

Within five minutes, the table was set and the meal ready to serve. Sara looked up at Rebecca and beamed. "This was fun. My grandma always says that two women in the kitchen are better than one."

"That's because Grandma likes you helping her." Adam had joined them.

Becca pivoted toward him. He filled the threshold, his gaze traveling over the scene, his eyes warming as he looked at her. "I enjoyed hearing your voices as I walked down the hall. Chattering away. It reminded me… Oh, it doesn't matter. Can you join us?"

He'd gone down memory lane again, but she wouldn't pry. Instead, she pointed at the spaghetti. "I'm going to be having a lot of pasta meals in the future."

His brow rose.

"Adam! I just got back from the rehab center, and I'm so happy."

She had his undivided attention. Sara's too. "Guess what!" Without waiting for an answer, she went on. "I'm going to be a bionic woman. I'm going to have a lightweight carbon fiber leg with bionic ankles and state-of-the-art microprocessors that are smarter than I am. They can sense what my leg will do—my gait—before it does it. Over a hundred times per second."

"Wow!" Adam opened his arms and she was there. In a nanosecond. His embrace tightened, his happiness for her absolute.

"It's a lot to absorb, but so exciting," she added, taking a step back, but his hand lingered on her waist.

"So does that mean your running worries are over?"

"I asked the same exact question in Boston." She peeked up at him. "I'll start real training as soon as I can.…I'm so glad I didn't give up, didn't get lazy with my exercises and therapy. I'm glad I've been walking the beach, too." Her throat tightened. "They said…they said…that the whole staff bet on me to win, place, and show. I'm not even sure what that means, but it sounded good."

She hadn't noticed her tears until Adam brushed them away. "Smart group. As smart as I am." He kissed her quickly. "Let's celebrate. I've got a bottle of wine somewhere."

"You know what else? Now that I think about it, the staff may have misled me. You know…bent the truth. Why should I be special? I have a feeling they cheered for every patient they had."

He grinned. "I'm sure they did. But it doesn't matter. You're a winner in our books, right, Sara?"

The child nodded. "Right."

"So, I'm filling the glasses," said Adam. "Wine for us. Juice for our girl." He raised his glass and clicked it with Becca's. "Here's to a winning future."

#

The Race for the Rescues committee had done a great job. Or so Becca thought. As participants gathered on the beach the Sunday morning of the July Fourth weekend, she and Adam greeted each runner, directed them to the fee collectors, and distributed number badges to wear in the race. Doc Rosen manned the first-aid station. The chief monitored the crowd. Bart Quinn held the microphone and gave directions.

The hum of anticipation, the mingling of the runners, the excitement of the observers all got to Becca.

"I'm running," she announced, holding up her hand before Adam could protest. "Just for a hundred yards or so… My everyday leg is good enough. I just have to."

"But I can't stay with you! I have to lead off…"

"It's okay. I'll be fine." She knew she couldn't keep up his pace…yet. But her heartbeat quickened at the thought of once more being in the thick of it.

"Stubborn." He walked away.

But when the race began, Becca had a shadow. Rachel Levine.

"You didn't think Adam was going to charge ahead and leave you alone, did you?" Rachel asked. "He and Jack may turn it into a 10K just for their own enjoyment."

"They can do whatever they want. And so can I. Sheesh, I'm not a baby. I thought you were my friend, too."

"I *am* your friend."

Becca studied the other woman, a swimmer, an athlete, a member of this community who had extended her hand from the beginning. At first she'd been gracious for Adam's sake, of course, but perhaps now, for Becca's, as well…? Looking at Rachel, she understood that the origin didn't matter. Rachel Levine was the real deal.

"Thank you."

The men and women gathered. The teens and kids gathered, too. All waiting for the starting gun. As appropriate, Adam made a welcome speech and kept it short.

"Although a rescue center in Pilgrim Cove was my idea, it cannot happen without you, every single one of you. All those creatures, lost or abandoned or who for whatever reason need a new home, should have a place to go. A safe place. Because you're all here, I know you feel as I do about this. So thank you for your support in helping get the center started. And now, if you're ready to show your mettle, follow me, and we'll all Race for the Rescues." His voice rose and echoed; the gathering applauded and moved behind him to the starting line.

Becca would have loved to take the lead with him. But she focused on her own one hundred yards. The length of a football field. A familiar distance. On the beach with an unlimited vista before her, however, a hundred yards seemed forever. She ran slowly, setting the pace, Rachel a half step behind.

Her brain was a microprocessor, registering every feeling, aware of every movement she made. Her leg worked well. She picked up the pace a fraction but couldn't get into that zone she was used to when the running was as smooth as silk. When she flew on autopilot. Today, her conscious mind was fully engaged. As she approached her hundred-yard mark, her residual limb started to burn.

"Uh-oh," she said, coming to a slow stop and facing Rachel. "We're going to have to walk back and take our time." Blisters? Burns? Infection? After being so careful for so long... She couldn't evaluate the damage until she got home and looked. Bad timing. Even a slow walk could make it worse.

"How about if we walk off the beach to the sidewalk, and I'll get my car and pick you up?" said Rachel.

"Where would you park? The streets are jammed." There was another alternative, one she hated to use. One she'd never used in public. "I have a wheelchair at the house. Can you call Laura to bring it up? The ROMEOs can manage the tables until we get back."

"Absolutely."

"I should never have tried it. Or I should have done a hundred feet, not yards. Adam will be mad. You and Laura are going out of your way..."

"Hold it right there," said Rachel. "Take it from one who's trained professionally in a sport. Sometimes training is about taking one step forward and two steps back. It's a constant evaluation and reevaluation. A constant process of adjustments, large and small. So, don't be so hard on yourself. You're in great shape. Today was a low point. Or a learning point. All athletes experience those."

Those high school students Rachel worked with were lucky to have her on their side. For the second time that morning, Becca said a heartfelt thank you.

"For what? I was telling the truth."

And that was the point that resonated. She'd recognized Becca as an athlete and spoken to her as one.

#

By the time the runners returned to the starting point, Becca was sitting at a table in a knee-length skirt, her crutches propped next to her, her wheelchair back at the house. Her smile never faltered. She made sure of that.

Adam stopped mid-stride as he approached her, his eyes missing nothing.

"I'm fine, I'm fine," she said, pre-empting him. "And you'd better get over there to Bart Quinn. He's got the local news reporter with him. Who knows what that old rogue is saying?"

He pointed a finger at her. "We'll talk later."

"Huh? I'm not your kid."

"Could've fooled me."

When later came, however, after the race, the dog parade at the soccer field, and after night settled over Pilgrim Cove, and after Adam and Sara had showered and returned to Sea View House, Becca's experience took second place to the crushing race results. In the middle of the kitchen table, checks and cash lay bundled into piles of hundreds. No matter how many times Adam and Becca counted, the numbers didn't lie. They'd fallen short of their financial goal. Disappointment hung in the air.

"I can't leave the expansion halfway done. Construction doesn't work that way. You either build it out or don't build at all." Adam's jaw was tight, his voice sharp. "Another setback."

Men didn't cry, but their feelings ran deep. Adam's sorrow and frustration showed, and Becca longed to help. "You're right. It's simply a setback. That's all it is. You can deposit these funds in the bank for now. We'll add to them after doing another event. Another fundraiser."

And if looks could kill...

"This is boring, Dad. Can I take Ginger and watch television inside?"

"Sure." Then he turned back to Becca.

"I know you mean well, Bec, but I'm working straight out. I've got two more greys coming this week. I've got no time..."

"But I have time. Maybe there are umbrella organizations for general rescue centers. Aren't there famous celebrities who are spokespeople for animals? I can do some research, and maybe we can apply for grants."

The metamorphosis that came over Adam amazed her. His expression softened, his eyes lit, a smile grew and lingered as he listened. Were her ideas so unusual?

He jogged to her side of the table, leaned over, and kissed her as if he had all the time in the world. "When I look at you, I don't even care about the money. It's you...that you offered...you would do all that for me? For this project? You have so much on your own plate now. How can you—"

She pulled him closer. Her lips met his once more, and she explored. The textures of his skin, mouth, tongue. The sweetness of giving and receiving. In his arms was exactly where she wanted to be. She knew he wanted the same.

"Adam…" she whispered. "I can get you the rest of it."

"Hmm? God, I wish Sara was with Katie tonight."

She giggled. "Me, too. But did you hear what I said? I can give you fifty thousand. That would get you over the top with some left over for operating costs."

He jerked back, and the air around her cooled. The atmosphere between them cooled, too.

"That money is yours," he said, each word deliberate and slow. "Even if we were married, I wouldn't use a dollar of it. Never bring it up again."

Her mouth fell open. Her thoughts whirled like children on a carousel. Adam would be Number One on her mother's Hit Parade. An honorable man. Unlike Angela, Becca had been attracted to an honorable man. She could hear her mom's voice. *Don't let him get away.* She could hear Bart's voice. *Grab the brass ring.*

No. And again, no. Love had to be a two-way street. A fifty-fifty partnership. She'd give her whole heart to Adam but would accept nothing less in return. Perhaps Adam wasn't the right one. *Even if we were married…?* He loved her. She knew it. Felt it. But without those three little words, any permanent union would be absurd. Not for her.

"I needed help this morning because of the blisters," she said. "You can't imagine how I hated being in that situation, but help came from my friends. Be careful not to fall on your pride, Adam. The rescue center is truly needed here. I imagine you have many abandoned pets when the summer folk leave. What will you do when another lost doggie is brought to your office?"

"I'll do what I always do. I'll manage."

She sighed. "I suppose you will. And I will, too."

#

Later that evening, Adam tucked Sara into bed, kissed her, and meandered to his office. A creature of habit, he supposed, always winding up the day at his desk at home. Shopping lists met his eye. Groceries. He was sure managing his life. His work life. His home life. What about his personal life?

Impatient with himself, he left the office and headed for his bedroom. Eileen's picture stood on the end table. He sat on the bed and slowly picked up the photograph.

"Hi, honey." His voice broke.

Her smile would remain effervescent forever. Her youth sparkled behind the glass cover. He'd lost her only five years ago, and yet it seemed a hundred years had gone by, and he, a hundred years older. He inhaled deeply.

"I've met someone, Eileen. She's brave and kind and loves Sara…and I know she loves me."

He traced her mouth, cheek, shoulder. And took another breath. "I didn't look for it. I never thought much about it…but with Rebecca, it wouldn't be a marriage of convenience. It would be the real thing. I love her, but I'm afraid. That's right. Your big, smart, strong husband is afraid. Because if I lost her like I lost you…"

And what would that do to Sara?

Shaking his head, he carefully placed the picture back on the table. Life on earth was finite. He certainly knew that. He was neck-deep in life-and-death issues with patients every day. But now he was the one in the spotlight. Scared and unsure. He couldn't live in the past but was afraid of jumping into the future. And the clock kept ticking.

CHAPTER FOURTEEN

A week after the race, the clinic door swung open with a thump, and Rebecca twisted herself on her stool to investigate.

Bart Quinn stood on the threshold, his face beaming as soon as he saw her. "So, there you are, lassie."

"And where else would I be on a weekday morning?" She found herself sitting taller, getting ready to match wits. The man's never-ending ideas and cunning required a worthy sparring partner.

"You are exactly right," he said, "exactly where you should be."

Not really. She was temping for Arlene. "I don't see a leash or a cage," she said. "So, what brings you here today, Mr. Quinn?"

"It's the boy-o." He nodded toward the back of the clinic. "All is not lost. I've been doing some talking to people." He leaned closer. "And I've got influence. Yes indeed, a l-o-t of influence with them. So you tell our boy-o back there not to worry. This town will have a first-rate animal rescue center or my name's not Bartholomew Quinn." His fist banged on the counter.

The guy was great entertainment. Becca went along with it. "I'll be sure to tell him. But he'll probably want some details…?" Hint—*she* wanted the details.

The man's pointer finger wiggle-waggled in front of her. "Not yet. Not ready yet. But it will be a big deal. I promise you that." He turned to go, then looked back. "What do the kids say now? TTYL. Talk to you later. That's it."

He sauntered out, leaving Rebecca chuckling. The man's heart was in the right place, as usual, but she shrugged off his grandiose scheme. She had one of her own. A straightforward, practical one—an anonymous donation.

She glanced at the calendar and realized that July was half-gone. Summer in Pilgrim Cove seemed like a very short season. Or maybe time flew because she was happy. Happier than she'd thought to be ever again. She began to hum as she worked.

Josie's phone call interrupted her lofty thoughts, just as Arlene showed up for her shift. "Hi! And hi. Can I call you back, Josie?… Yes, yes I'll hurry."

She left the clinic and, once in the car, auto-dialed her cousin. Josie's reason for calling could be anything. Wedding details? Shopping for dresses? A visit to Sea View House? The possibilities were endless.

"I found the perfect apartment," began Josie. "One large bedroom. First floor. And a backyard. Small, but better than nothing. And it's near the hospital. I'm afraid it won't last long on the market, Becca. The question is, should I take it?"

Becca's mind had to readjust. The apartment search had been lost in her flurry of activity in Pilgrim Cove. "What's the rent?"

"More than we'd hoped, but not over the top." She named the figure.

"Take it!" said Becca. "But see if we can stall. Maybe you can give her a month's rent to hold it for us until next week. I'm due for a fitting on Tuesday at the rehab center."

"What if she wants me to sign a lease right now?"

"It's too late for me to get there today," she said, leaning back in her seat. "And tomorrow I promised Sara to go to her softball game. She joined a summer team with Katie and Casey. I think it's good for her."

"Who? Oh, the other little girl I met? Hmm... I have to say, Bec, you sound like you've found a new life out there."

Maybe. Or maybe not. "Not sure, Josie. But if I have to make a decision now…"

She drummed her fingers on the steering wheel. With the "bionic" leg, she might be able to return to her career at full capacity. Too much at risk in not following through. "Do it. Sign a lease if you have to."

"I'll keep it to six months or less. Or I'll think of something else."

"Thanks, cuz."

"Before I go," she said, "here's a reminder from Nick: Keep the money in the bank." She'd lowered her pitch an octave. "No cars. No trips. No houses. No nothing. Don't let it go to your head."

Becca started to laugh. "Are you kidding? Doesn't he know how we grew up? Well, especially me."

Josie reclaimed her own higher tone. "He means you should lie low until you're ready to talk to a financial advisor. He'll set up an appointment if you'd like—and then hold a gun to the person's head."

"You're the best, both of you." She turned the key and started the car. "Go talk to the landlady and don't be concerned about my bank account. It's healthy."

It was still healthy after she went online and tracked her recent withdrawal and deposit as a blind check into the Pilgrim Cove Rescue Center fund.

#

"Softball seems like serious business," said Becca, scanning the crowded parking lot behind the middle school where the field was located.

"Weekends are family times, especially in the summer," Adam replied. "We've got weather issues the rest of the year."

They got out of the car just as another vehicle parked near them. "Katie and her dad are here," said Sara. She put on her cap and glove and danced over to her friend. "Come on, let's go find our team."

Katie turned toward her own dad. "Can I go, or do you need help?"

Becca watched with interest. She'd seen Jason Parker from a distance at the Lobster Pot but never met him up close. Tall, lean, with dark hair and eyes and a strong step, the man certainly looked capable of taking care of himself and anyone else.

"I think I can handle your little sister all by myself," he replied with a grin. "Go have fun, you two. We'll be watching from the bleachers." He waved the girls down toward the field, then glanced at Becca and Adam. "Good morning."

Adam extended his hand. "Morning." He glanced between Becca and the other man. "Have you two met?"

Jason stepped over. "Only in passing, I'm afraid. How are you, Ms. Hart?"

She liked him. His enthusiastic handshake couldn't have been friendlier, maybe because of the girls. Becca had made Katie welcome at Sea View House. The famous pop musician and composer had returned to

Pilgrim Cove after many years, reignited the flame with Lila, and met his older daughter for the first time. Becca had gotten the details in dribs and drabs.

Just as she was about to reply, another sound filled the air. The sound of a baby's cries. Jason flipped his car keys to Adam. "Pop the trunk, will ya?"

He opened the back door of his vehicle and lifted Rosemary out, still strapped into her car seat.

"Oh, my goodness, she's beautiful." Becca stared at the infant as though spellbound. "I rarely get to see newborns."

"I see them all the time," boasted Adam. "Just not human ones."

"Ergo, no diaper duty," said Jason, putting the car seat on the ground and spreading out a changing pad in the back of the SUV. The dad efficiently removed the baby from the car seat and laid her down on the foam pad. Becca was drawn to the infant like a magnet, stroking the tiny hand and instinctively making cooing noises, ignoring Jason while he manipulated the diaper and salve.

The baby turned toward the sound of her voice. And blinked. Then sighed. "Ooh…my," whispered Becca, swallowing hard. "She's…she's…a miracle. Fingers, toes. That cute little mouth. Just perfect."

A butterfly kiss brushed against her temple, and she heard Adam's low rumble in her ear. "So are you, Becca. So are you."

#

Covered with sweat after putting herself through her daily exercises, Becca answered her ringing cell. It had an impatient sound to her ears, probably because she'd ignored it earlier. She smiled when she saw who was at the other end.

"Hi, Adam."

"You sound breathless," he began.

"Just finished working out. I need a shower."

"Then I'll be quick. I got good news today." His excitement came through the airwaves. "You were right, Bec! An angel showed up, a true animal lover, a big donor. I can start construction now. Maybe it was someone at the race. Someone who needed extra time to consider the benefits to the community. But whoever he or she was…well, I hope I can thank them one day."

Without warning, her breath caught, tears welled, and she felt her heart breaking. "That's fantastic! I'm so happy for you. You really deserve it. But now I've gotta go clean up. We'll talk more later, okay?"

She let the shower wash over her, the water hot, her tears joining the flow. Sharp pains pulsed through her stomach. Her great idea of a week ago now felt like a lie. What had she been thinking? He hadn't wanted her money. He'd been more than clear on the subject. And a relationship had to be based on trust. On truth. In the end, her grand gesture would boomerang. Fifty thousand secrets couldn't be held at bay forever. Whatever love and regard he had for her would disappear.

#

Adam whistled a lively tune as he opened the clinic door the next morning, Sara at his side, giggling.

"You sound happy," she said, "but I don't know the words."

"There are no words, sweetie. I'm making it up."

"Nope. Katie's dad makes up songs. You take care of pets. And now we can take care of lots more."

He leaned down to hug her, reminding himself that children often preferred concrete rules. No shades of gray for Sara, except for the coats of many colors on the rescued hounds.

Becca wasn't at the reception desk, but as he walked by, a call came in. Peggy got to it first and handed him the phone. "It's Becca."

"Need a ride?" he asked. The woman had never been late to work. "Car problem?"

"No. I just forgot to tell you I'm going into Boston today and won't be at work. I just called Arlene. She'll try to get in earlier than usual."

"Going for a fitting?" The only reason she'd be forgetful is her excitement over the new prosthetics. A closetful, she liked to say. Choices.

"Actually, no. The fitting's tomorrow. I'm going to see an apartment Josie found for us."

His head jerked back as though she'd slapped his face. For a moment, he couldn't speak. "Just like that? Without saying anything?" He could have kicked himself. He hadn't been paying enough attention. He'd just assumed... He'd been afraid...

"Boston's not that far, and...well, good apartments are hard to find."

Not as hard as the right person. "Funny coincidence, Rebecca. I have business in Boston today myself. Which ferry are you taking?"

"More greys, Adam? Oh, my. You'll have three or four now. Unless I take another one for a little while."

The right person... "Which ferry, Bec?"

"Ten o'clock."

"See you at the dock."

He turned to Peggy. "Cancel all my appointments and reschedule." He pulled out his mobile and auto-dialed Lila Parker. "Can you or Jason pick up Sara at camp and take her home with you? Something important came up. Something good. I'll tell you later. And don't say a word, not one word, to your grandfather!"

He returned to the house and rambled through his closet. She liked the lime-green dress shirt. He put it on and rolled up the sleeves. What the hell was he doing? She knew what he looked like. And he didn't even have a ring. He changed his slacks, too, and transferred his wallet. If all went well, they'd shop in Boston. *If...*

He stared at the photo on his end table. "Wish me luck, Eileen. Wish me luck."

#

Adam pulled his car into the ferry lot and spotted Rebecca halfway to the dock. He quickly caught up and put his arm around her.

"You look wonderful, Adam. Please don't tell me you're fetching more dogs wearing that beautiful shirt." Her light comment coupled with a wide smile would have thrown anyone else off track. But her eyes—those dark brown eyes were now shadowed instead of gleaming with humor.

"What's wrong, Bec?"

She started, then beamed up at him. "Not a thing. According to Josie, I'm going to love the new place. Reasonable rent for the area, near the hospital. What more could I want?"

He hadn't gotten to the crux of her problem, but she'd given him an opening he couldn't ignore. "I was sort of hoping that you wanted the same thing I did."

She froze. And to his horror, tears rolled down her cheeks as quickly as Niagara's waterfall. A fist squeezed his heart, then tore his insides to ribbons. Was she sick?

"Come here." He led her to an empty spot along the railing, away from the other passengers. "Have the doctors told you something else? A setback?"

"No, no. Worse than that."

Impossible. "I love you, Rebecca. If you're healthy, everything else is secondary."

She cupped his cheek. "Oh, Adam. I love you so much, and I do want the same thing you do."

The fist eased, and his heart fluttered to life again. He began to speak, but she held up her hand. "I've done something you're going to hate me for. And we can't have a relationship like that."

The dark drama under a bright sunshiny sky seemed so wrong. "C'mon, Becca. Your imagination is rivaling Sara's. How can I hate someone I love so much?"

"Because I lied."

He paused. Okay. He hadn't been expecting that. "About what?"

She remained silent but continued to stare at him, and like a lightning strike to the brain, he knew.

"You're the angel. The financial angel."

She nodded. "I made the donation. You work so hard, and I love you so much. I wanted to help." Her tears began again. "Strangers helped me. So I thought, why couldn't I help Adam?"

Her thinking was muddled. He gently pulled her close to him, against his chest. Let her tears and makeup get all over his damn shirt. Who cared? "Because of you, I'm such a lucky man. You loved me enough to make a mistake. So you're not perfect. And neither am I."

She'd calmed down. Hopefully, she'd been listening. He kissed her forehead, cheeks, mouth. Sweet, sweet lips.

"The money goes back into your account, of course, and we'll figure out something else for the center. It might take a little longer, that's all." And suddenly, the longer time frame didn't seem like failure. With Rebecca at his side, Greys and Strays would get done somehow. But was she really in his life for the long haul?

"Hold on to the rail, sweetheart, because I'm getting down on one knee."

"Oh, my God, Adam, you don't have to…"

"I want to." He wanted to give her the romance every woman dreamed of, and he was a man who paid attention to a woman's dreams. A plus for being a husband once before.

"I love you, Rebecca. But you should know that I'm not perfect, either. I wanted to do everything right, but I waited until I almost lost you. And I don't even have a ring to give you right now."

"You couldn't lose me…"

"Will you marry me and Sara? We both love you so much."

"Of course I will. I love you both. Now get up before you lose your balance and we both slip overboard."

He did, and for his reward, she wrapped her arms around his neck and pulled him toward her. Their kiss sizzled from the get-go, mellowed for an instant, and returned to fireworks level in no time.

"Forget the apartment!" he muttered. "Let's go buy the ring right now. I want to tell the world—and especially Pilgrim Cove—that we are walking down the aisle."

"A perfect proposal," she said, kissing him again. "Whether it's an aisle, a sandy beach, or a cement sidewalk, as long as we always walk home together, our lives will be perfect enough for me."

"Amen."

EPILOGUE:

The Boston Globe –
Sunday, September 1

MARATHON VICTIM WALKS DOWN THE
AISLE—
CONCERT RAISES MONEY FOR ONE FUND
BOSTON

Rebecca Hart doesn't think of herself as a victim. "I was just in the wrong place at the wrong time," she says. But not even a determined woman like Ms. Hart could deflect an exploding bomb last April near the finish line of the Boston Marathon. She lost her left leg above the knee, but you'd never guess by watching her walk or run. You'd never guess that one of her fashionable shoes with the two-inch heels is attached to a prosthetic foot. You'd never guess that a shattered life became whole this summer when Ms. Hart set up housekeeping in Pilgrim Cove, MA, a town that's "just a finger in the ocean."

"Pilgrim Cove is now my home. I met my wonderful husband, Adam, there and, as a bonus, fell in love with his ten-year-old daughter. I made friends that will be with me for a lifetime."

Luckily for One Fund Boston, one of Ms. Hart's new friends is musician Jason Parker, a Pilgrim Cove native. The songwriter and piano man performed a sold-out concert last night at the high school football field. A concert at the Boston Garden will come later. Parker was backed up by his talented family—brother Matt Parker, daughter Katie and nephews Brian and Casey. The concert was arranged by Mr. Bartholomew Quinn, a prominent citizen of Pilgrim Cove.

Ten percent of the gate will be donated to Greys and Strays, an animal rescue project of Adam Fielding, DVM and the new Mrs. Rebecca Hart Fielding. "As a runner, I identified with the retired greyhounds Adam was caring for and placing into loving homes. The difference is the word *retired*. The sweet greys have more than earned their rest. But I will train for another marathon."

Rebecca Hart is Boston Strong.

#

With a deep sigh of satisfaction, Bartholomew Quinn folded the article and placed it in his desk drawer. He'd add it to the Sea View House Journal. In a plastic sheet. The old-fashioned way. No computer records for him! A person should hold the book, heft it on a lap to read. And pass it down to the next generation. Who would be responsible for preserving the magic of Sea View House on a computer? None of the ROMEOs, that was certain. Well, he'd be around for a good long time yet making sure future tenants would be worthy. And speaking of… Didn't he have an appointment…?

He thumbed through his calendar. Ah, yes. Another potential candidate would be arriving soon. A photographer who'd seen too much trouble through his lens. The Captain's Quarters would suit him fine. The place had elbow room. He turned to another entry. The kindergarten teacher, Joy MacKenzie, had made an appointment. He didn't know what she had in mind— perhaps to buy instead of rent? Whatever the reason, he looked forward to the visit. The petite lass was always entertaining.

He rubbed his hands together, a broad smile on his face. An interesting autumn lay ahead, and life in Pilgrim Cove couldn't be better.

SEA VIEW HOUSE JOURNAL

(Pilgrim Cove Series)

From Laura McCloud Parker—I arrived at Sea View House in March, looking for a place to catch my breath and get on with life. I'd just lost my mom and completed my own breast cancer treatment, one event right after the other. The first person I met in Pilgrim Cove, besides Bart Quinn, was Matt Parker. And the first part of him I saw was his jeans and work boots, sticking out from beneath my kitchen sink. "Hand me the wrench," he said, thinking I was his son. How could I have known then that living in this *House on the Beach* would forever change my life? Bart says it's a magical place. I'm not arguing.....

From Shelley Anderson Stone—The children and I arrived at Sea View House on Memorial Day weekend. Divorce hurts everybody, and we all needed time to recover. Bart Quinn had given us the large apartment downstairs called the Captain's Quarters. I had no idea that Daniel Stone would be living upstairs in the Crow's Nest, dealing with his own grief. I also had no idea he would rock my world—in the very best of ways—and that we'd provide each other with a second chance at love. Looking back, I can say that season was *No Ordinary Summer* for any of us....

From Daniel Stone—Read Shelley's account. Here's my P.S.: If there's any magic at all, it was provided by

Jesse, my golden retriever. Two little kids and a golden?
Pure magic.

From Rachel Goodman Levine—Like a prodigal
daughter, I returned to my hometown of Pilgrim Cove in
the fall, trying to prove myself as an assistant principal
of the high school. Instead of living with my folks, I
landed at Sea View House. I wasn't alone there. Thank
you, Bart Quinn! Marine biologist Jack Levine had
settled into the Crow's Nest. My initial delight turned to
dismay when Jack joined my teaching staff, breaking all
the rules with his unorthodox methods. And getting me
into trouble. It was then the magic happened. The
discovery. The love. Somehow, we *Reluctant
Housemates* are now housemates forever right here in
Pilgrim Cove....

From Jack Levine—Read Rachel's story. All I'll say is:
magic, my eye! Sure, I'll admit that sailors are a
superstitious bunch. But here's what really happened:
My boat went missing and shook her up. It wasn't
magic. It was a miracle! All of it. So believe what you
want.

From Jason Parker—I came back after nine years
because I couldn't outrun the pain. Prom night. A car
wreck. My twin brother gone. Our music gone with him.
Except not. I've got platinum behind me, and what does
it mean? Nothing without the folks I love. Less than
nothing without Lila Sullivan. She's always been the
one, the only one for me. Bless Bart Quinn for lending
me Sea View House. My daughter was conceived there a
long time ago. But I didn't know anything about her all
those years. Folks might call Katie *The Daughter He*

Never Knew, and they'd be right. But I know her now. As for her mom and me...? Sea View House came through for us again. Our wedding took place right there. I believe in the magic. I believe in happily ever after. If that's not love, what is?

From Lila Sullivan Parker—Read Jason's account. All I'll add is that the right girl for lovely Adam Fielding is still out there. Jason's return saved Adam and me from a tepid marriage of convenience. We both deserved more. My money's on Adam and Sea View House.

(Sea View House Series)

From Rebecca Hart Fielding—It's summer again, a year since the last entry in this journal. The magic is still here. In this place, in this town, in its people. After the Boston Marathon, I arrived at Sea View House with no expectations except to focus on rehab. I wanted to hide, but that's impossible in Pilgrim Cove. In a nutshell, I met Adam in a bar. A nice bar at The Wayside Inn. It was definitely *not* love at first sight. But something changed along the way.

From Adam Fielding—We fell in love. That's what happened. That's the magic everyone talks about. No woo-woo. No smoke and mirrors. Scientists don't believe in that stuff. When Becca came to Sea View House, all she wanted to do was walk again. She was stubborn. She was proud. And she was determined to remain the athlete she'd always been. I'm happy to say that *Her Long Walk Home* brought her straight into my arms.

EXCERPT FROM
HER PICTURE-PERFECT FAMILY
(SEA VIEW HOUSE SERIES BOOK TWO)

CHAPTER ONE

When he heard the quick footsteps head toward his office, Bartholomew Quinn rose from his comfortable leather chair, ready to meet his visitor. His knee ached with the effort. "Don't have time for the arthritis," he mumbled, limping across the room, "no matter how many years behind me. And blast this weather for causing it." He opened his door and glanced at the petite young woman, his grin rivaling the Cheshire Cat's. He forgot about his pain.

Rain dripped from the hood of her bright red jacket. A red umbrella— closed and dry—hung from her wrist next to a large, colorful tote bag. His gaze drifted lower. She wore sandals; her feet were soaked. "Ach, lassie, come in, come in. You're wet through and through."

"But I'm right on time," she announced, cocking her head. "Aren't I?"

Quinn's laughter fed his soul while filling the room. "That you are, my girl. That you are." The kindergarten teacher had become a favorite of everyone in Pilgrim Cove. Quite an accomplishment in only two years. From the beginning, Bart thought she seemed barely older than her young charges. He wasn't alone in that. But she had the knack of making each child feel special, which, in his opinion, was the secret of her success in the classroom.

"You're not only on time, Joy MacKenzie, but a sight for sore eyes, too. So, let's get you dry."

She hung her jacket over a hook on the coat stand and shook out her hair. Short, blonde, and feathery. "Will winter come early, I wonder? It's almost Labor Day, and school's starting within the week. We simply cannot build snow people before we pick apples in the orchard. Well…I suppose we can, but that's topsy-turvy."

Bart understood that by "we," she meant her class. If there was an adventure to be had for the children, Joy was in the middle of it. The parents loved her for it and helped out.

"Always autumn before winter. That's the way of it," said Bart. "You'll pick those apples soon." He gestured to the visitor's chair in front of his desk. "Make yourself comfortable." He watched as she tucked one foot under her and sat.

In his own chair now, he leaned forward. "So how can Quinn Real Estate and Property Management help you?"

She dug into her tote bag. "It's the strangest thing," she said, pulling out an envelope. "I've been evicted. Thrown out. Mrs. Williams needs my apartment for her newly married daughter." She handed the letter to him.

He perused the correspondence. It didn't take long. "The note's dated a month ago. Why didn't…? Ahh— now I remember. You've been away visiting your family on Cape Cod."

For one fraction of a second, her blue eyes darkened, a shadow hovered. "That's right. I was on vacation. In Provincetown. I forgot to forward the mail, and it just…just piled up."

Something was amiss. Sooner or later, Bart would find out what—he took pride in keeping up with all of Pilgrim Cove's residents—but the wee gal needed help now. And he was the one who could solve her problem.

"Rent or buy?" he asked.

"Oh…I wish I could buy. I love this town so much, I'd live here forever. But even I know what's possible and impossible." She leaned over the desk. "Mr. Quinn, a teacher doesn't earn a king's ransom, but I get such satisfaction from my classes, I sometimes wonder if I should pay the school board instead of them paying me for being with the children."

"Joy Mackenzie!" he exclaimed, banging a fist on the desk. "Loving your profession is no small thing. We need more like you in our schools. Not that Pilgrim Cove has bad schools, no sirree. High school scores are soaring since Rachel Levine came back to town."

Joy nodded. "We have good staff on all levels. Hmm…maybe not everyone, but strong in general." She took his hand. "My folks would love me to move back to Provincetown. They're getting more vocal about it. So can you work some magic and find me a home right away?"

He didn't know much about her folks, some artsy people he'd heard, but it seemed Joy would certainly rather stay put in Pilgrim Cove.

"So, it's magic you want? Well, not to worry. The house I'm thinking of comes with its own built-in magic. But it's only temporary, mind you, until we find a new place for you to hang your hat."

"With school starting next week, I just need some breathing room. A couple of months will be fine. So where will it be?"

"You'll have a view of the ocean, the cry of the gulls, and a beach front you can't normally afford. Sea View House is the place for you. Right now, the upstairs apartment is available. The price is right, too."

He named a low figure, and her mouth fell open. "Sea View House is part of the William Adams Foundation," he explained. "And he was related to John Adams, our second president. The house is leased on a sliding scale. Perhaps you can save some money while you're there...?" Hint. Hint. He wondered at the lack of financial literacy with some young people.

She beamed. "Great idea. Thank you very much. I know where it is—on Beach Street. Everyone in Pilgrim Cove knows about Sea View House."

"But no one knows exactly how it operates, except for the ROMEOs. And we don't talk."

She put both feet down and leaned back in her chair. A smile broke out. "Ahh—Mr. Quinn, the ROMEOs. However, you're not retired or old. But you're a man for sure. And with your daughters in the restaurant business, you probably do eat out a lot. For that, I don't blame you. Not at all."

Clever. Clever. His band of brothers, the Retired Old Men Eating Out, couldn't have been described more succinctly than Joyful MacKenzie had done. Right on the money, too.

"I count myself lucky to be your tenant," said Joy.

"Good. Good. There's just one more thing."

Her brow furrowed for a second. "Whatever it is, I can handle it."

"While you're in the Crow's Nest upstairs, there will be another tenant downstairs in the Captain's Quarters. Separate entrances, of course."

Her quick smile returned. "That's even better. I'll enjoy the company. My mom says I've never met a person I didn't like. So what's her name?"

"Not her. *Him*. His name is Logan Nash." Quinn's thoughts spun like scenes in a kaleidoscope. He hadn't planned this one in advance, but he'd take advantage of what fell into his lap. He had an oversupply of those gut feelings people talked about. And those feelings were bubbling up right now. Joy MacKenzie would be perfect for the troubled photographer.

He rubbed his hands together in anticipation. Autumn was about to begin in Pilgrim Cove. He just knew the magic would begin again, too.

#

Logan Nash stood at the water's edge, face lifted to the gray sky. "Come on, clouds! Open up and let 'er rip."

The saturated clouds responded to his plea, and his laughter ping-ponged through the heavy drops. Alone on the beach, Logan spread his arms wide, shook his head, his shaggy mane now soaked through to his scalp. Cool and wet rain—he loved it. Such a relief from the hot, dry heat and winds of Iraq and Afghanistan.

His body clenched. His lids shut tight. *Forget about it. Not your problem anymore.* His job right now was to relax and recover. An easy prescription to write. Not so easy to implement. He'd had no idea how to forget the last two years of his life, or at least deal with them.

Embedded with the military, but not part of it, he was on his own now. A house at the beach seemed to be a reasonable start, especially since he'd sublet his place in Boston, a small condo that provided him a stateside address. This new place, Sea View House, had elbow room! And Pilgrim Cove, snuggled between the Atlantic

Ocean and Pilgrim Bay, provided an environment completely different from the one he'd left behind.

Lightning flashed, and he started jogging toward the big house. His wet shirt clung to his skin; his khaki shorts would need days to dry. When thunder boomed, his heart lurched, his muscles tensed. He forced himself not to drop in place. Instead, he sprinted toward the big gray house. After reaching the back porch, he collapsed onto a redwood chair. Every part of him trembled, from head to foot, inside and out.

"Idiot! No bombs. No landmines. Just Thor with his bowling balls." Yeah. That's all. A story. Relax.

"Thor? Why, I love Greek mythology, too."

He jumped and twirled. The voice came from another wooden chair not five feet away. From a child in a red raincoat, the hood framing a sweet face. He kept his distance.

"Are you lost? Does your mother know you're here?" His raspy voice reminded him that he'd been silent all day. No phone calls. No people in his face. Just the way he liked it. He cleared his throat.

"My...my mother? Lost?" The girl grinned, then laughed as though he'd told a very funny joke. "I'm sorry, Mr. Nash, but I seem to have the advantage." She rose and walked closer, arm extended. "I'm your new upstairs neighbor, Joy MacKenzie."

He stood but ignored her gesture. "Quinn didn't say anything about renting out the Crow's Nest."

She looked at her empty hand, tilted her head back until her eyes met his. "Did I catch you at a bad time?"

Her meaning was obvious, but he didn't want to worry about etiquette, niceties, or putting on a show. Any time would be a bad time. He wanted his privacy. Which was why he'd jumped at renting Sea View House. No neighbors on either side after the season, which ended this weekend on Labor Day. And Bart Quinn had said the apartment upstairs was empty.

"I'm a rude SOB, so you'd better find somewhere else to live." He headed into the house.

HELLO FROM LINDA

Dear Reader:

Thank you so much for choosing to read *Her Long Walk Home*. I hope you enjoyed your visit to Pilgrim Cove and the first story in my new *Sea View House* series. For some of you, *Her Long Walk Home* was an introduction to this cozy beach town. For others, it was a reunion with old friends from the *Pilgrim Cove* series. In either case, I hope the story kept you turning the pages as Rebecca Hart and Adam Fielding found their way home together by following their hearts.

If you enjoyed this book, please help others find it so they can discover Linda Barrett books, too. Here's what you can do:

• Write an honest review and post it on Amazon, Barnes & Noble, iBooks, GoodReads or any of your favorite book sites
• Keep up with me at my website at *www.linda-barrett.com* to find out about

upcoming books and what's going on in the writing world

• Sign up for my newsletter at *http://lindabarrett.authornewsletters.com/?p=subscribe&id=3*

• Join me on Facebook at: *https://www.facebook.com/linda.barrett.353*

• Tell your friends! The best book recommendations come from friends because we trust them.

I truly appreciate your help in getting the word out about *Her Long Walk Home* and my other novels, which are listed here and available electronically and in print.

Many thanks,
Linda

LINDA BARRETT BOOKS

NOVELS—ROMANCE:

(Sea View House Series)
Her Long Walk Home, 2015 (Bk. 1)
Her Picture-Perfect Family, 2015 (Bk. 2)

(Harlequin Books, Superromance)
Quarterback Daddy, 2010
Summer at the Lake, 2009
Houseful of Strangers, 2007
A Man of Honor, 2006

(Pilgrim Cove Series - Harlequin Books)
The House on the Beach, 2004 (Bk. 1)
No Ordinary Summer, 2004 (Bk. 2)
Reluctant Housemates, 2005 (Bk. 3)
The Daughter He Never Knew, 2005 (Bk. 4)

The Inn at Oak Creek, 2003
The Apple Orchard, 2002
True-Blue Texan, 2001
Love, Money and Amanda Shaw, 2001

NOVELS—WOMEN'S FICTION:

The Soldier and the Rose, 2014
Family Interrupted, 2013

SHORT NOVELLA:

Man of the House, 2013 (part of *Celebrate Romance*
anthology with four other authors)

MEMOIR:

*HOPEFULLY EVER AFTER: Breast Cancer, Life and
Me,* 2013 (true story about surviving breast cancer twice)

Printed in Great Britain
by Amazon